cM

M000232164

UNTIL IT HAPPENS TO YOU

"Journey of Understanding, Acceptance, Forgiveness and Love"
I think about how long I've managed
To persevere in spite of,
Yet because of!
I do know that
I was meant
To be here.
I do know that there
are people who
really do love me.
Unconditionally.
I now realize that the ones
Who I thought loved me for me,
Who really only loved me
Conditionally,
Were all a necessary,
Part of my journey.
I understand now that my
Experiences; the good,
And the not so good,
May also be part of the
Blueprint of
Someone else's life.
It just might be yours!
Today my journey begins....
S. K. Mitchell

UNTIL IT HAPPENS TO YOU

"Journey of Understanding, Acceptance, Forgiveness and Love"

S. K. Mitchell

THANK GOD
FOR BLESSING ME WITH
THE
STRENGTH, WISDOM,
AND
COURAGE
TO
FINALLY SHARE
MY STORY.

Until It Happens To You
"Journey of Understanding, Acceptance, Forgiveness and Love"
Published by S. K. Yokopomi Publishing
Email: skor9610@gmail.com

Written by S. K. Mitchell

Copyright © 2017 by S. K. Mitchell

All Rights Reserved. No part of this book may be reproduced or transmitted in any form or by any means, electronic or mechanical, including photo copying and recording, or by any information storage and retrieval system, without permission in writing from the publisher, except for brief quotations and critical reviews or articles.

ISBN—13: 978-0692056646
ISBN—10: 0692056645

Cover Design: Jamel Kornegay/Rebecca Adams Designs
Cover Photo: T. E. Mitchell

Printed in the United States

DEDICATION

To my loving husband for his unwavering love and support. My prayer is for us to continue on our journey together for always, because I'm not quite sure where I would be without you.

To our wonderful children for always believing that mommy can do whatever she puts her heart into. Know that I am so very proud of you, and pray that God continues to bless each of you with the desires of your heart.

To my family and friends, who have been as close as family; for allowing me to be part of your journey, and for always being with me along mine, without question.

*Love and Continued Blessings
From My Heart to Yours!*

FOREWARD... *The Time is Now*

Like many others, I have watched movies that were so absorbing that I felt as though I was actually a member of the cast. I've watched those with levels of intensity so high that I was left talking nonstop about the characters; what should have happened; and what I would or would not have done, if that had been me.

It's always been almost second nature for me when it comes to analyzing dysfunction and coming up with recommendations about one situation or another. After all, I have lived what I, and most others, have perceived to be as normal of a life as one can have. Lately, though, I have come to realize that those who are on the outside looking in, seem to regard my journey as being slightly different than normal. But not for reasons of which I have had control, nor for those I would have opted for if given a choice.

I had no idea that my life would one day change, and without warning. Before I was even born, and without regard for how I might one day feel, it was decided that my life was to be lived as a lie. Similar to the performers in a top-rated stage play, the roles of the characters in my life were acted out effortlessly. Unbeknownst to me I, too, played my part very well. I must have been conditioned at birth, because I never imagined life to be anything other than the way it was.

I had no clue that my existence had been completely manipulated by those who had selfish agendas, using me as a pawn and my mere presence as a token along the way. I remain confident, however, that there were yet a few with compassion so strong that they

iv

allowed themselves to be tugged in directions that wouldn't have otherwise been preferred. Though they became major players in the overall scheme of my life, my heart tells me that their plan was never to participate in a plot that, if revealed, would hurt me in any form or fashion. They only wanted to love and support each of us, unconditionally, as they helped to protect the sanity of the one they felt would lose it, if she didn't have her way.

As I share my feelings and emotions about my life in general, I'm often told that my life sounds so much like a movie that I should write a book. So, one day I decided to take a closer look at myself in hopes to see what others had seen. And it worked. I was indeed transparent. It was all clear. I'm not living the perfect life. In fact, things appear to be a whole lot less than perfect, though my performance is impeccable.

The unassuming would never have imagined some of the experiences that I have had. Those things that make up my very existence. Finally, able to see what others who knew me best could see in me, I made the decision at that point to start writing things down. Not journaling necessarily, just simply writing notes here and there, which allowed me to actually view my life on paper.

This process was okay at first, but quickly became somewhat mundane. It was like a never-ending task, with disjointed words on paper and no clear meaning. It took a while for me to understand that this type of writing should be more specific, so I began to compose letters instead, addressed personally, yet never intended for delivery. I would jot things down as thoughts came to mind. Summer after summer, when I had the most time free from the major responsibilities of life, I tried effortlessly to make sense of it all. Until one day I realized that I was making this process more difficult than it had to be. There had to be a better way to do this. And then one day it hit me. The impossible became possible.

I have shared one or two letters, which contained extreme sentiment, only with those whom I felt could be trusted with my innermost feelings and emotions. Not to be judged. Seeking only to find some form of reassurance or validation of my feelings. I needed to know that I was seeing things clearly and to make sure that I was not being overly sensitive in certain situations. Reactions were sometimes tearful, with tender words of love and support for me, ending with what has become familiar words: "Wow, this is like a movie. You really need to write a book!"

As my letter writing grew in intensity, given one situation or another, I began to think as others did. I had become the main character of a movie. It was time to share with others, the story of my life!

(NOTE: Although this book is written as a personal account of various aspects of my life, names of all individuals and places of encounters have been altered and somewhat fictionalized. Situations have been slightly embellished and are used for illustrative purposes only. Any resemblance noted is to be considered circumstantial.

CHAPTER ONE.... *My Life at A Glance*

Not long ago, I found out that I was not given a name at birth. My original birth certificate, as recorded in the vital records of the state in which I was born, bears only the four-letter word "girl" on the line where a name should appear. When I decided to openly share the experiences I have faced during my life thus far, I decided that my first step would be to change my name from "girl" to "Rebecca". I was born in a large metropolitan area up north, and educated in the mid-western part of the country for my elementary and most of my high school years.

Growing up as an only child, I had all of what I wanted and sometimes all of what someone else may have desired. My dad wanted me to have the world. He didn't want me to grow up poor like he did. He wanted nothing but the best for me, and I had just that. I wasn't a brat, though. At least I didn't think so. I was always happy to share anything I had.

Recent occurrences in my life have forced me to pause and take some time to think. Time to reflect and try to make sense of several hurtful situations that I have encountered in relationships with people who once meant the world to me. There are always at least two sides to every story, so from my own individual perspective I am saying that these happenings

1

were beyond my control. I understand that life goes on, regardless, yet moving on has not been an easy task.

Continuing to look as though I have it all together, when I'm really falling apart on the inside, increases my level of anxiety with risks I should not have to endure. Feelings of emptiness and loneliness make matters worse when I think about yesterday, and the people I could never before have imagined living my life without. Some have gone on to glory so there's no fault, but others are still here yet hold a presence in my life that is pretty much nonexistent. There are some who are standing by pretending to care for me, but are secretly watching and waiting for the day that I crumble. I recall one of my aunts asking me if anything bad ever happens to me or my children; and if so, to please let her know.

Contrary to those wishing for me some form of despair, there remain a handful of others who genuinely love and sincerely care for me. It is because of them that I have mastered a façade, as a way to keep them from worry. Waking up day after day to put on a mask, go to work, perform at home as a wife, mother, grandmother, friend, neighbor, mentor; going about all of the normal things one does in a day without ever letting on that you're really not okay. Just doing what I do, holding it in, until such time as I reach that uncontrollable boiling point.

Immediate family maintain a watchful eye, with their front row seat of my life, quick to respond when they notice me in what appears to be too deep of thought. They know the look, that distinct expression on my face which leads them to the conclusion that something lurks within and I'm just about to explode.

Internalizing has landed me in the emergency room on more than one occasion, with an anxiety attack as the diagnosis. My husband recently confessed to me that he has been concerned about my mental stability and overall sanity for a number of years. Though I'm not the one, in the story of my life, who was always expected to lose it, the question of my sanity yet remains. I've tried to blame irrational behavior on changes with my hormones, since that always seems to be the most logical explanation for behavioral changes in women. But I have to be honest with myself at this point. It's not the hormones. It's my life.

After having so many to tell me that I should write a book about my life, I decided to give it a try. The interesting thing about those requests is that they come from those with only a glimpse of the surface of my existence. The core, though, is what I believe will be the most useful. My life experiences are, no doubt, like that of so many others, so I expect many to see themselves in the pages that follow. I believe from my heart

3

that we are here on this earth to help others, and that we should use our talents in that endeavor as best we can.

I believe in the possibility that just as we have individual hand and foot prints, people are also born with a certain number of words to use. Quite honestly, as I don't want mine wasted, I make every attempt to use them as carefully as possible. Being human, I might waste a few from time to time, but the ones I choose to share at this point in my life might help to save others a few of theirs along the way. And that works for me.

Hopefully someone who is experiencing a situation that they don't see their way out of, will find themselves on one of the pages, and realize that they will be just fine. And hopefully there will be one who will admit to being on the other end of the pain, the heartache, or the disregard, and will decide that enough is enough, and want to make things right. Before it's too late.

By no means do I profess to having all of the answers, but as I recall my life, my journey, the paths I've taken willingly and unwillingly, I now have a better *understanding*. I have now *accepted* those things that have had a profound impact on my life. From the depths of my heart, I have finally *forgiven* all of those who have caused the hurt, the pain and the disregard that I have felt for so long.

Please note, however, that coupled with my forgiveness, is a new course of life. One that puts me on a path that keeps me from ever again being hurt by those causing the pain. I'm not foolish enough to think that I won't, again, encounter situations or people that will hurt my feelings from time to time. It's just that I will do my very best to avoid those situations, those relationships bearing even the slightest resemblance to what I have painfully endured thus far. I don't believe there is any harm to doing that. There can't be anything wrong with protecting myself from the emotional chaos that is, ultimately, not in my best interest.

I'm not saying that during my journey, I have only been on the receiving end of disappointment. In my lifetime, I am honest enough to admit that I have made some mistakes and have hurt others along the way. Some of the decisions I have made may have caused some discord, but hardly ever have I purposefully done things to negatively affect the lives of anyone else. When so, I would often find myself overcompensating with efforts to make it right.

The things that weigh heaviest on my mind and heart, and those for which I have had to work the hardest to accept and forgive, have happened without warning and appeared with a great surprise. The impact so profound that I had to question myself, and what I could have possible done to cause these things to happen.

Those I have met in my adult life, and have since become closer to me than the family I grew up with, tell me time and time again that it's not my fault. They find it necessary to constantly remind me of the fact that I am a good person, and that those who have created the circumstances that have caused such a major disruption in my family life, are in fact the ones to blame.

In fact, there may be a kind of evil that causes these individuals to constantly wear blinders, never acknowledging their role in the dysfunction which plagues their relationship with me, and perhaps with a few others as well.

I have never been a tattletale. I've never been that person who wants to run to tell on someone else. Like what someone has done to me, or the things they have said about me that are completely untrue. I've mastered the art of holding it all in. Protecting the offender, I suppose. And protecting others who I don't want to experience disappointment upon hearing that the ones they hold at such high regard are not so perfect after all. I always seem to put the feelings of others before my own, a practice that is hardly ever in my best interest.

Seems that no matter what happens, everything ends up being my fault, since I choose not to run and tell anyone who will listen when someone steps on my toes. I just keep it to myself. Even when I don't know there is a situation with my name attached to it, like when a lie has been told, that too, ends up being something I am expected to apologize or ask forgiveness for. For no fault of my own, each situation becomes part of my life story.

I've often wondered if the expectation is that I'm exempt from pain, because I'm perceived as being so strong? Am I the one who always has to turn the other cheek, even when the act against myself, or those closest to me, is so blatant in the eyes of everyone except a select few? Well, there comes a day when a person just can't take it anymore. When enough is enough! When you actually get lower than a snake's belly and you are forced to stop and reevaluate your own existence. Yes, the pain for me at this point in my life is just that great. The hurt is really that bad. But no one is ever to know. I'm too confident a person for that. I try to never cry in front of anyone, never reveal my pain or weakness. I cover my eyes attempting to hide what hurts so badly.

Forced to have thick skin from as early as I can remember; a characteristic that ended up being essential for me in my struggle to maintain my sanity as a child, has given me a rather tough exterior. Not just at home, but also within the communities in which I've lived. I was taught to be strong and to never let "them" know that their actions bothered me.

I recall being teased about the shape of my body. I was tall, slender, flat chested, and had a protruded derriere. I can recall quite vividly, the time when a group of girls walked behind me laughing about how they could sit a bowl on my butt and it probably wouldn't fall off. I continued to walk as though they were invisible and without hurrying my pace. It was important for me to let them know, nonverbally, that I was not afraid of them or their words. There was never a direct altercation between them and me. No words. Actions only.

Another time that forced me to use that tough skin I had developed was on a bus ride home from school. That same group of girls sat in seats nearby and must have decided that I would be the joke of the day, as they decided to point, make silly comments, and laugh at the shoes I was wearing. These were actually brand-new shoes; and, yes, they were different. Because I liked them and wanted them, my dad gave me the money to purchase those different looking shoes just in time to wear on my first day of high school. I always got whatever I wanted, whenever I wanted it.

I didn't react to those girls then either. I continued on my way, never looking back, and never uttering a word of concern then or later over their remarks. They had no idea of just how insignificant they were to me. I continued to wear my shoes, they obviously found someone else to taunt or laugh at, as I made them completely invisible for the rest of my time at that school. Actions only. Again, no words necessary.

At my favorite place, my grandma's house, there were six boys, four older and two who were younger. With them I had no issues whatsoever. Since I was the only girl, my grandfather made it a point to teach me early on, how to use either my fist or the biggest stick I could find, to fight off anyone who bothered me.

My dad followed that lead by enrolling me in self-defense classes once I was ten years old. I never wanted to fight anyone but boys since they were who I was used to being around. Girl drama never got a rise out of me. I'm sure it made me appear somewhat aloof, but I really didn't care. They didn't have a clue, and I had nothing to prove to anyone. I had thick skin, and I could definitely defend myself, if or when necessary. For the most part, I chose silence as my defense, which is likely when I developed the act of holding things in. Maybe that wasn't the best thing after all.

I told myself that I could never be hurt by anyone, and I meant just that. Especially not by that emotional kind of hurt. The kind of hurt that no one can see, though it has the potential to hurt to the core of your being. From as early as I can remember, I made a vow with myself that no one would ever know how their actions or words bothered me. I could handle it. Keep things to myself. Tell no one.

Once I became an adult, I started to think about the overall impact of my past and the affect it has had on me as a person, not just emotionally, but also physically. I have always had very sensitive skin but never imagined that emotions could be a culprit. But once I really stopped to give it serious thought, I was able to make a direct correlation between the itching and hives, and my emotions.

As a child, my skin would begin to itch or I would sometimes start to turn red in spots and break out in hives for no apparent reason. This would happen mostly when my feelings were hurt, when I felt all alone, or at random times that carry no real explanation. It was rather hard to explain, and remains so to this today. My family would just say that I had sensitive skin and tell the other children not to touch me because they might make me whelp up.

While at my grandmother's house down south, the younger boys would sometimes tease and run into me, scratching my arm just to watch the transformation. An ashy scratch mark would turn into a bumpy, red raised mark that would eventually disappear. Sometimes I would chase the boys and hit them with a stick or fly swatter once I caught up with them. At other times, I would just sit and imagine life with a sister.

I do recall my mother taking me to a doctor at one point during my childhood to get checked out, since the whelps and hives were beginning to occur much more frequently. Having no real medical explanation to help us understand what was going on with my skin, the doctor simply performed an in-office test using a little cardboard tongue suppressor. He stood behind me, asked me to spell my name slowly, as he used that instrument to outline my name on my back.

Just like clockwork, my skin turned red and began to raise, displaying my name on my back as I knew it would. The doctor was amazed and offered little, other than to suggest that I not scratch too hard when I had an itch because that alone might make it worse. I still have that issue with my skin, but since I understand now that much of it is likely related to my nerves, I try my very best to avoid the triggers.

In a nutshell, this basically means that it is high time for me to start controlling those who have caused me the type of emotional stress that has the potential to leave marks on my back. And perhaps it's also high time for me to let those people know just how their actions have truly affected me. It's time for me to open up and use my words before I allow another to pounce on the strings at the core of my soul and rip away at what's left of my heart.

I should have paid more attention to what my dad told me. Repeatedly. The love for you will never be like the love shown towards others. He said for me to always remember, in cases of indifference, that my feelings would never be considered, because the others "can never do no wrong!"

In my more than half century of living, I have done my best to handle what life throws my way. Lately, though, I find myself getting tired. I feel as though the energy source that drives the level of my emotional tolerance has been drained. To help myself to heal, I feel it's best to analyze my life from conception to present day.

During this process, I will be forced to make a few assumptions, as certain facts remain a mystery. Secrets and sleeping dogs are ever present. My disclaimer is that as I attempt to analyze, process, or figure it all out, it is important for me to state that it is not my intent to use my words to hurt anyone at all. This is all about me. There are actually quite a few incidents that I could write about, but only those situations that have had the most profound impact on my existence will be included in my analysis.

This is not about vengeance, or humiliation, or even an eye for an eye. It's just me doing my best to connect the pieces that form the puzzle of my existence. I'll do my very best to find the pieces that are missing and place them where they fit best in the grand scheme of my life. Perhaps I'll find that those things have always existed but have just been down for a nap, like those sleeping dogs that are supposed to lie forever. What shall I do if the missing pieces are found and all begin to fit together? And if sleeping dogs are made to lie, what do I do if those dogs one day awaken?

The most safe and serene time and place for me to reveal my thoughts has always been when I am sitting with a clear view of the never-ending ocean. The water provides a sense of calm that allows me to feel and openly express my emotions without concern or thought of anything other than those things that are inside of me. As I hear the roaring of the waves and splashing as they each hit the banks of sand, it reminds me of letting go.

As situations in my life have soared to unimaginable heights, the waves represent that calm release. Letting go of those things that have churned endlessly in my mind. For years. This is my time. Like those waves, I have reached capacity, and can finally let go!

CHAPTER TWO.... *The Story Begins*

"You just can't make this stuff up!" Words familiar to Rebecca's ears, often used by her husband, following one of the many issues she seemed to face with some member of her family, time and time again.

Growing up as an only child, she always had nothing but the best. Her dad made it a point to make sure she had whatever his little girl wanted, whenever she wanted it, with no concern of what it was or how much it cost. Her mom's initial goal was to make sure that her daughter had more than she had as a child, until such time as resentment began to set in. As one of the many children who lived in a small home in a rural town in the south, her mom often yearned for the material things to validate her existence; a characteristic that resulted in her living almost a lifetime of artificial existence.

The husband Rebecca's mom chose was the perfect one to help secure her fairy tale of a life. This would appear to have been ideal for the cute little girl, adorned with the cutest clothes, fine wavy hair, and fat little cheeks with deep-set dimples. A story with this beginning would seem to have chapters full of joy, devoid of complications associated with any form of dysfunction. Unfortunately, Rebecca's life as a child was quite the opposite.   But in spite of the subtleties she endured as a child, she held firm to her desire of wanting to help others once she grew up.

It became second nature for Rebecca to use whatever she had; her talents, her resources, and her network of friends to help others.   Until she noticed that enough was never enough. Until she noticed the scars on her back, resulting from literal stabbings that occurred without her even knowing she was under attack.   Until the day came when she started to feel the pain from the piercings deep inside of her heart.   Jealousy. Envy. Spite. Bitterness. Apparent hatred. Coming from the ones she had grown up with from the time she entered the world; the only family she had ever known; the only family she could ever trust; those who were supposed to be part of her life forever; those she had always loved wholeheartedly, her mother included.

As if many years of hiding the emotional pain weren't enough, Rebecca was hit with a blow that surpassed anything she had ever endured. The ultimate deceit. Life as she knew it was all one big lie. She was a secret. Did everyone know, except the now very grown up Rebecca, and is that the reason she was now so disregarded and avoided by the only family she had ever known and loved? She had to decide whether to get angry and "react" when things got out of control, or take the high road and silently embrace what she was told by her grandmother over thirty years ago, that sleeping dogs were made to lie. Or should she accept what she has always known, that God does things in His own time, in His own way, and according to His purpose?

As Rebecca struggles with never ending disappointment from her loved ones, and pain from the memories of her past, she has no idea that the roads of *understanding, acceptance,* and *forgiveness* are roads that must be traveled if she is ever to locate the key that unlocks the void that has existed in her heart for as long as she could remember. This key could one day open the door to an unconditional life, and to the *love* from a family that she yearns and deserves. This is all true. This is all real. You just can't make this stuff up!

CHAPTER THREE.... *Introducing Rebecca*

Her mother's name is Liza. Her grandmother has always been called Mama Gee by most, but to this little girl, she was Grammi. Her earliest memories of her life are rather vague. But she has been able to take bits and pieces of what she has heard here and there, add them to the memories of her own that refuse to fade, and come up with an understanding of her life from the beginning. Her journey. Her life. Her filling in the blanks. Her name is Rebecca.

When I stopped to take a glance at my life, the quick snapshot reveals that I'm really not much different from anyone else. We have each had one reason or another to analyze ourselves in hopes of revealing a specific strength or to acknowledge and rectify a weakness.

If we are really to be honest with ourselves, we will understand that the path we are on has been predestined and efforts to do things our way don't always go the way we would like. But it is hard. Difficult to stay the course when so many other things are more appealing. And if we have a big heart, we allow others to redirect us for their own selfish reasons which we then rationalize even more. The balance isn't easy, and when it tips too far to the left, we can end up with feelings that are damaged beyond repair. I pause now to see how I arrived at this point in my life, from where my journey began on that bus ride to Waters Edge when I was just five-weeks old.

It was actually one particular Thursday, when I stopped to really give some thought to my life. That day was significant because it was during the month and year that I turned half of a century old! It was my fiftieth birthday. I started that day the same as I do on each day that I am blessed to wake. By first saying "Thank You", just as soon as my feet hit the floor. My day began earlier than usual on this particular day. I couldn't help but to wonder if that was a sign that I was going to start waking that early from then on, much like Grammi used to do for as long as I could remember. She would wake up with the chickens. I realized later that they were very noisy creatures, with their loud crowing; and perhaps, by divine design, they were actually nature's alarm clock.

On that very special morning, I began to think about my life from day one, recognizing the significance of our days. Each of us will have birthdays for as long as we are on this earth, and each is definitely unique. However, I believe that certain ones have just a little bit more significance than others.

Of course, the day we are born, we are met with smiling faces, especially from the ones who were used as the vessels to get us here. We venture on year after year after that, growing and developing our own individual personalities, marking milestones along the way. Perhaps most talked about is year number two. By then we have usually learned to walk, talk, and get into any and everything within our reach.

I'm not sure how many of us can remember that particular year. My earliest memories begin a tad bit later. I do remember being told, however, that I was never really treated like an actual baby, because I didn't act like one. I wasn't a whiny, clingy toddler. I didn't play a lot with cute little toys, because I was mostly around children who were older, and there weren't really many toys at my grandmother's house anyway. I did have a doll or two, and a few stuffed animals.

After the age of two, the next major milestone is perhaps year five, when we start school for the first time; although I started when I was four years old because my birthday came a few weeks after the first day of school. In most cases, an earlier start was allowed if the child exhibited a level of maturity expected for that grade level.

I was always very advanced for my age, so I would end up in the smart/advanced classes, and would also earn the designation as teacher's pet. I remember when I was in the first grade, when others were down for a nap, I was able to stay up with the teacher to help her with little projects. That was great for me because I never liked to take naps anyway.

There was no real transition from elementary to middle school, since the school I attended was for kindergarten through eighth grade. Birthdays from year to year, would generally be acknowledged, to include only immediate family and a friend or two, with cake and ice cream but no major fanfare.

Teenage years bring the next milestones and a little bit extra. For me, it was around age thirteen was that I started my extra, believing that I knew more than my parents and just about any other adult on the planet earth. Any resistance to that fact by anyone, resulted in my next stage of passage, "rebellion". This was mostly projected towards my mother, since she and I were usually the only ones in the house.

That type of behavior from me was likely heightened, because to me it appeared as though the older I became, the less my mother seemed to like me. Initially, I thought that the relationship we had was the way it was supposed to be for mothers and daughters, and that the term "rebellious" was synonymous with names of all teenagers, not just me. Especially teenage girls. I heard it so much from my mother.

"Rebecca, you need to stop being so rebellious." "You're going to get enough of being so rebellious." "You are the most ungrateful, rebellious kid I have ever seen." "I'm going to tell Mama Gee just how rebellious you are and how awful you treat me." Over and over again that's what I would hear if I messed up in the least.

Quite frankly, I didn't really know what the word meant because I was so very young when it was introduced, but I dared not ask. My experience with my mother whenever I tried to ask about something I didn't understand was met with the response of, "How dare you question me. You know that you know better than to question authority. I have done my best to teach you. You are the most rebellious kid I have ever seen."

It was easier for me to just assume that rebellion had something to do with not wanting to wash the dishes, iron her clothes, or take out the trash, since my resistance to chores was when she used it the most. Overall, my mother's attitude towards me made life more difficult during those years, mainly because I was an only child and had no one else in the house to help share the brunt of her frustrations.

I could always tell when my mother was in one of her moods and didn't care to have me around, for whatever reason. I would just go to my room. She would remain downstairs and soon after, I would hear her pick up the phone, dial a number, and have endless conversations with whomever was on the other end. That seemed to be just about all that she enjoyed. Sometimes I would sneak back downstairs quietly so she wouldn't hear me, and listen to what she was saying. I could always tell when the conversation was about to end. That would be the cue for me to scurry back upstairs to my room to avoid getting caught listening to grown folk talk.

After a while, my mom would come upstairs to remind me that it was time to turn off the light, say my prayers, and go to sleep. I would do as I was told, praying for everyone in the whole wide world and a special request for my mother to not be so sad. I never referred to her as being mean or anything like that. I just figured that she was short in the area of patience with me because she wanted to go back home to Mama Gee's like I did. And also like me, maybe she didn't like living in that town either.

Anyway, I was a teenager and had no problem letting anyone know how intelligent I was, or why my way was always the right way. My grandparents, however, were exempt from all of this. My maternal grandmother, especially. She's the only one who always understood me. When I was fourteen, though I had spent the formative years of my life, each summer and most holidays down south with her, I told her that I might not be back once I turned fifteen, because I was going to get a job. Grammi chuckled at the thought of her sweet Ria, as only she called me, working on anyone's job. All she knew was that I had spent a great portion of my life with her and she couldn't fathom things being any different. I did end up back down south, for the entire year, and for a different set of circumstances.

Anyway, sweet sixteen came and went for me. Unlike most of my peers in the city where I lived with my parents, there was really nothing major for me to look forward to during this milestone year, since I had received my driver's license at the age of fifteen and had already attended a prom. One of my uncles (by marriage), who had adored me from the time he first laid eyes on me, made sure that I learned how to drive and could do so legally before I returned back home at the end of the summer. This all happened during a year of my life that I made the decision to move away, for a reason that is really too embarrassing to mention at this point.

Anyway, the very day that I returned back home to my parents to finish out my last year of high school, my dad said, "Lets go"! And off we went to pick up the red and white automobile, with AM/FM radio, that I requested as a condition of my coming back to live with them.

Even after I returned home, I continued my rebellious ways, or so my mom said, and she made every attempt to take my keys from me. She said it was because I didn't follow her rules, but I know it was really because she was mad because my dad bought me a car in the first place. I didn't use the car to hang out with boys, only with my friends, who often sat patiently on their front porch, waiting for the red and white chariot to arrive. We would pile into that car as tightly as we could. Comfort was never an issue.

Once I turned seventeen, I eagerly awaited the end of the school year because I would be off to college and free from all of the attitudes directed towards me, and the arguments between a miserable mother and an often absent, Friday through Monday, father. I would be FREE. A thought that stayed with me until the day I left for college.

My journey continued on to the age of twenty-one, an age which marked the time in which I was expected to be legally responsible for myself. For some of my peers, perhaps that was the case, but that wasn't the way things worked out for me! I had not yet finished college because I decided to quit, and I didn't have a job. So, the dreaded return home was inevitable, since my parents hadn't completely given up on me for dropping out of college. I was received back home with open arms from my dad and with a look of disdain on the face of my mom. According to the way she projected herself around me, she had all the answers by the time she was the age I was then, so it was apparent that I had a problem. At least that had always been my perception.

The few times I cried out to my mom because of confusion, uncertainty, and agony regarding the course my life seemed to be taking, I was always met with "Get yourself together, kid. I have never had the opportunities you have"! So, I stopped sharing my feelings with her, and learned to maintain the thick skin that I had developed early on, in order to handle anything that came my way. Any situation. Any challenge. Any obstacle. Any hurt. Any pain. Any disappointment. From any relationship, especially if it involved one of her nine siblings. Her family. Also, mine when it was convenient.

So here I am now, all grown up, and trying to figure myself out. During many sleepless nights, I sometimes find myself in deep thought as I struggle to make sense of my life in its current state, and particularly how I came to be. It's like the journey goes on and on without making much sense. But why not? I understand that others may have the same question, but for me, a lot seems to come full circle back to the relationship I have with my mother. Resulting in more questions than can be answered at one sitting.

What were the circumstances surrounding my birth? Was there love for the thought of me before conception? Did my birth represent the end for my mother? Did my mere existence cause her to have a life that was full of disappointment, hurt and pain? If given the opportunity to go back in time, would she have made a different choice?

Abortion? Adoption? Abandonment? Does she feel as though she lost the best years of her life because of my existence? Did she regret making sacrifices that caused her to lose more than she bargained for? Were they really sacrifices, or the resulting consequences of her selfishness? And would she ever stop blaming me for her not having the story book life of which she had always dreamed?

All and all, as I look over the journey that I've taken thus far, I do hope to find the answers to some of those questions. And I know what most are thinking: at this point in my life, why on earth do I even care? What will the answers do to change the course of my life, and is that ultimately the desire of my heart?

Putting together the fragments of my life as the pages turn will require me to add a little bit here and there, particularly where certain pieces don't really fit. It will also require third person analysis during those times when I wouldn't have been present. I'm hoping that this will help me to *understand* why things happened; *accept* the ones involved, directly and indirectly, for who they are; *forgive* the ones who have hurt me in any way; and, *love* them all regardless, even if it's with Grammi's long-handled spoon.

Chapter Four…. *Meet My Mother*

Referred to by her daughter, Rebecca, as "my mother" most of the time, Liza reluctantly journeyed back home, and with no intention of staying. Waiting patiently for the bus to arrive was Liza's stepfather, Butch, the person responsible for her abrupt departure from the place she thought she would live for all of her life. And now here she comes, returning with a child. Something that was never included in the life that she had imagined for herself. What will people think of her now? Maybe they won't know the baby is hers if she doesn't show her face. Maybe they'll think that Mama Gee had gone and had another baby. She seemed to have one every year and a half anyway. Her youngest had just turned three years old a few months prior, so it was conceivable.

After dropping passengers off in the not so big city of Kinville, the bus continued its south bound trek to the final stop along its route, to a small town with a population of less than fifteen hundred. Comprised mostly of several generations of about ten different families. The bus rounded the last curve leading up to the small Waters Edge city limits sign, considered by the locals as what separated them from the rest of the world. Most of the people in Waters Edge had never ventured beyond that one small sign even though they often fantasized about just how far that road on the other side would actually take them. Having no earthly idea that their town was connected to a major highway, separating not just counties and small towns, but many cities and states in that entire region of the country.

Little did baby Rebecca know, but this bus ride marked the beginning of what would be a roller coaster ride of life for her, and for no fault of her own. Her mother, Liza, didn't realize that the one to meet them would be the one who was responsible for her running away.

Everyone in Waters Edge and surrounding counties knew that Butch was a man who always got his way. His presence was felt as soon as he entered a room. The ladies in the town would smile as he neared, hoping for one of the strong and warm hugs he was known for. Sometimes those hugs led to a bit more than they should. And his advances were rarely denied. Men would joke and laugh at Butch's beckoning, but secretly had little desire for him to be around. But because he was nearly six and a half feet tall, with broad shoulders and a thick waistline, his sarcastic humor and rough housing was hardly ever challenged. Though his size and boisterous nature gained him a tremendous amount of popularity outside of his home, those with whom he lived felt a totally different presence where he was around. The rigid, tense, and cold home life with his wife and nine children left a lot to be desired.

As Liza held onto her newborn baby girl, she gazed out of the window, finding herself in a deep trance as she recalled the events that led up to her escape from the place she had always expected to be her final resting place. It had been less than a year now since Liza had returned home from a date with her beau, Chaz Mayes, III, only to find Butch pacing the front of the old wooden house she had shared with her immediate family, which consisted of Butch, her mother, her eight siblings, and very often, whoever else needed a temporary safe haven.

Liza's mother, who most knew as Mama Gee, was known to have a home with an open door to each one of her own brothers and sisters, along with neighboring kinfolk, and also those seeking immediate refuge. It seemed a regular occurrence for her to have women, along with their children, to show up at her door at odd hours of the night with only the clothes on their backs, no food, and little or no money. Most were running away from abusive spouses, even though more likely than not, they would always return.

Mama Gee met Butch when Liza was just a toddler. Even though she had finished the highest level of schooling possible at that time, and had managed to escape what seemed the norm of getting pregnant at an early age, she still managed to get pregnant out of wedlock. She found it hard to resist the tall, handsome and charismatic star athlete, Daniel C. Lane who was best known by the townies as "DJ". Born the 12th of 18 children to the Lane family, DJ remained consistent his whole entire life. He was kind. He was generous. He was likeable. He was Liza's biological father and Rebecca's maternal grandfather.

As the bus neared the end of the its route for its passengers before turning around to head back to the big city, Liza's mind traveled way back in time. She saw the pretty young girl who yearned to live in the big house with her real father, her stepmother, and her half-sister. Though she wasn't really interested in being under the same roof as Nora's mother, Amelia, who never seemed to care much for Liza or Mama Gee, she still wanted the attention from her father and the material things he had to offer. Her mind rested on the jealousy she had for the life that her sister, Nora, had being a privileged member of the Lane family.

Nora was only two years older than Liza, and was also born out of wedlock. But no one seemed to care about that at all. It wasn't until DJ's proposal to Mama Gee was declined, that he even agreed to marry Amelia, the mother of his first-born child. DJ and Amelia never had any other children, with no explanation offered. Living in the big house as an only child, Nora was spoiled rotten, having everything she wanted and then some.

It was never a secret that she was Liza's older sister. Instead of protecting her the way older siblings would usually, Nora taunted Liza for being poor and living in a house with, what she referred to as, a bunch of pitiful looking children. They both lived on the same lane so they all rode the bus to school together. Nora was always first to board the school bus so she would eagerly wait for the bus to stop at the end of the driveway where Liza and her younger school aged siblings would board each weekday morning.

Teasing would begin as soon as Liza stepped foot on the bus. Once, Nora actually poked fun, utterly humiliating Liza for having on a dress that was one she no longer wanted. "Hey sissy pants, even though I was kind enough to let you have that dress you're wearing, I hope you know that it will never look as good on you as it did on me when I wore it."

When she heard that snide remark from her sister, Liza simply rolled her eyes, took her seat on the bus next to her favorite cousin, and vowed never to be seen wearing that dress again. She wanted to burn it as soon as she got home, but knew that she would get a beating if ever caught doing that. As hard as it was for her family to get anything at all, Mama Gee would not tolerate the destruction of anything that could be of use to the other children.

Nora was very aware of the fact that, unlike her, there weren't many other children who could boast about having material things. But she did her share. And although her behavior was neither condoned nor tolerated by her dad, Mrs. Amelia would often smirk when Nora told her of the cruel things she would often say to her only sibling. Nora was very attractive and loved being known as the daughter of a man whose family lineage was considered to be among the wealthiest in the town. Not only did Nora's parents own a big two-story home with a wrap-around porch and two huge barns, they also had to their credit, a fair share of land and livestock.

It was no secret that Liza was envious of her sister, felt no attachment to her dad, and was disgusted by her mom, all at the same time. She basically accepted her fate of having to live this kind of life forever, since she couldn't foresee the possibility of leaving home to pursue anything better. The fact that she would have to spend her entire life helping her mother to care for all of the children she seemed to keep having was pretty much etched in stone. And for that, she secretly resented each and every one of them.

Liza would never have imagined that the one day in December, when she was given permission to go out on a date with Chaz, a person whom she had admired from afar since she was just a little girl, and with whom she could only dream of sharing life with, was a day that would end up haunting her for the rest of her natural born life. That one special day is what pretty much sealed the deal for the rest of Liza's life, making it forever impossible for her to achieve the glamorous lifestyle she often fantasized, with the one man she would always love.

Though Liza thought he would never be interested in someone like her, a person who was from a family who had very little as compared to others, she was totally mistaken. When the day finally came for Chaz to muster up enough courage to speak to her after his high school graduation, Liza decided to shield her embarrassment and allow this charming fellow into her personal space. It was no secret that Chaz was interested in being more than just a face in the crowd of fellas who admired the pretty and shapely young girl who always had hair with waves and curls to frame her face ever so perfectly.

Chaz started to visit regularly after their first date, mostly on Sundays after church, since that was when everyone looked his or her very best, and were on their best behavior. In their small community, everything stopped on the day of the Sabbath and time was strictly devoted to family, friends, food, and fellowship. Most children were allowed to run and play after church services had ended, and were exempt from all of their chores. The older girls still had to help with dinner, of course, but that was even more relaxing and enjoyable on this day. Probably the main reason that Liza preferred Chaz to visit on a Sunday, was because this was the one day of the week that Mama Gee would have the kind of food prepared that Liza was not ashamed to eat.

Having a house full of mouths to feed, her mother welcomed just about anything that anyone offered. Food that would help her to provide meals for her family, as well as the others who found themselves seated at her table for one reason or another, was always appreciated. It was not uncommon to see a sack on the front porch of Mama Gee's house, that contained scraps that were left over after a hog or cow had been slaughtered. Liza had to help Mama separate the contents that would surely be used during the weekdays to help make a pot of stew, season vegetables, or even be used for medicinal purposes. On Sundays, though, one or two of the chickens from their own chicken coop would be sacrificed as the main dish along with a big pot of collard greens, corn on the cob, mashed potatoes, corn bread and a delicious four-layer cake.

Lately, on those rare times that she could invite company over, Chaz was always her first choice. Liza looked forward to their time together after Sunday dinner was over. The two would take a stroll down the lane to have a bit of privacy from all of the chatter of the children, or from those who might stop by just to say hello and to hopefully be offered a taste of Mama Gee's, mouth-watering, dessert of the day. She was known at church to have the absolute best sweet potato pie, chocolate layer cake, and pineapple coconut cake on the planet. And although she had several mouths to feed, she always had an extra piece, or two, for guests.

As they walked slowly to savor every moment together, holding hands and swinging them back and forth with each step, Liza would have private thoughts of how life would be if she lived in the big city with Chaz. They would have a nice place to live, and enjoy fine dining and trips to the theatre. She would have the finest of clothes and would be envied by her friends for being the beautiful apple of Chaz's eye. He would spoil her with love and affection and anything else she could ever dream of having. The world would belong to the two of them alone, and her life in Waters Edge would become a memory of a life she wanted to forget.

Liza always felt inferior and as though others looked down on her because her family was poor. The shame and resentment she felt kept her from inviting anyone over to visit, even though her mother encouraged her to have a friend over every once and while. Mama Gee knew that her oldest child was slightly different from the others. She knew that Liza harbored resentment towards her because of the way in which they lived, and because of the number of children to whom she gave birth to after marrying Butch.

Though he was never comfortable with the visits from Chaz, Butch didn't say much during those Sunday visits because he knew that Liza wouldn't dare do anything less than ladylike on the Lord's day. It wasn't that Butch had anything against Chaz. He was just a very stern father and refused to let any of his girls end up with a man like him. Therefore, Butch made it his priority to do whatever he could to keep Liza and her sisters, Leah and Beth from becoming tainted.

Though Mama Gee was about as perfect as one could be, and though he said that he loved her, Butch didn't forget that his wife was tainted when he got her, having already birthed a child out of wedlock. He justified his actions towards the girls by saying that she had not given them the best example to follow. This hurt Mama Gee to the core because she really loved DJ, the father of her first born, and had planned to be with him, but could not go against her own mother's wishes. So, she ended up with Butch instead.

It had been about two weeks since Chaz had visited, so he asked permission to take Liza out to see a movie one evening. Mama Gee thought Chaz to be a nice fella so she said that it would be fine as long as he had her home before sunset. After quite an enjoyable evening out together watching a movie with one of Liza's favorite actresses in it, the two arrived back before sunset just as they were told. Chaz was from a nice, God fearing family, and had several sisters of his own so he knew how important it was to be a gentleman and respectful of parents' rules, no matter how old one was.

With his eye on the clock to be sure that they arrived before curfew, Butch watched as the car Chaz was driving slowed at the end of the lane. Moments after the car stopped, Butch rushed to the passenger side of the car. No sooner than Chaz had leaned over to give Liza a soft kiss and a gentle hug, Butch yanked open the door, pulling a startled Liza from the car. He was yelling obscenities as he beat her with a rod as they made their way down the lane to the old house.

Chaz watched in shock, and though he wanted to help, he knew his place so he quickly put the car in reverse and high tailed it off of their property and down the road into the darkness. He didn't want to make matters worse for Liza by hanging around, knowing that his presence was the cause of her pain. Chaz had heard from his own parents, and cautioned that Butch was known around town to be a hot head, and for him to not be one of few people to cross his path.

As Liza screamed and cried for Mama Gee to help her, she promised herself that if she lived to see another day, she would not spend one more night under the same roof as Butch.

She was tired of running, tired of hiding in closets and under beds when he was angry and looking for someone to lash out at. She also knew that Butch was not afraid to do whatever he had to do in order to get his point across. There had been stories told around town about how Butch had nearly killed a member of his own family because he felt he had been disrespected in public, which was really the main reason he was so feared.

Once they were inside of the house, Butch hit Liza a few more times. Once he finished his ranting about Liza being a slut and how she was going to end up just like her mother, with a house full of chullin, he did what he always did. He said a few mean words to his wife, poured himself a drink of liquor, picked up his truck keys and left. Where he went was unbeknownst to the children, but Mama Gee knew. She always knew.

All of the other children and babies that Mama Gee had birthed for Butch, appeared from hiding once they knew he was way out of sight. They were all terrified of him and cringed whenever he spoke, fearing that a wrong move might result in a beating. As she would always, their big sister, Leah, gave the children a sign letting them know that it was safe for them to come out of hiding. The babies ran to Mama Gee for comfort as the older children gathered at the foot of Liza's cot while she silently sobbed and prayed for a way to escape the nightmare she had been living for the past nineteen years.

As the babies clung to their dear Mama Gee, and though they were infants and toddlers, they understood that their sister had been beaten. They saw the tears on their older siblings' faces, and felt their mom's heart beat with fear of what might happen next. From across the room, Mama Gee could tell from the look in her firstborn's eyes, that enough was enough!

CHAPTER FIVE... *Liza's Escape*

Peter received word that his sister was trying to reach him so he quickly found his way to the closest house on the block that had a phone. Peter was Mama Gee's youngest brother who was raised by an uncle after the untimely passing of their mother.

After the passing of their mother, most of Mama Gee's siblings were old enough to make it on their own. Peter was the youngest and a decision had to be made about who was to care for him. Mama Gee had married before their mother passed away, and already had a house full of children to care for, so an uncle whose wife was unable to bear children, offered to take young Peter in as their own. Even though the environment was stable and he had all the comforts of home he spent a lot of time with his sister and her children.

Peter was a tall, handsome fella who had the women in the small town of Waters Edge and the neighboring town of Kinville, crooning at his feet on any given day of the week. On the days that he was dressed in his slacks and loafers with his hair slicked down and brushed to the side, showing off the waves that made him look very distinguished, he was sure to have his pick. Since he had conquered most of the local women, Peter was excited to see how he would be received by the ladies in the big city, where several of his older brothers, and some others from his home town, now lived. As soon as he was of age, he made his move.

Dialing the number that he was given to reach his sister, made Peter nervous. He knew that his oldest niece was having a hard time living in the old house with all of the children, and the seemingly harsh rules set forth by her stepfather. Hoping that the call was not news that something had happened to Liza, as she had always been his favorite, caused a level of anxiousness that made his complexion change, and sweat to form on his forehead as the phone started to ring.

Close in age, the two were pretty much inseparable as children, and both took it very hard when his momma, her grandmother, passed away. Peter as the baby, and Liza as the first grandchild; were both very cute children having features much like their family matriarch, and were both spoiled at her feet. Liza often thought that her stepfather resented her because she looked so different from the other children. And although she appeared to be a mirror image of her grandmother, Liza actually resembled her biological father and his family the most.

Liza would never openly admit this, but she probably resented her paternal family about as much as Butch did. She thought it unfair that as a mere child herself, she not only had to help take care of the other children, but she was often given the hardest chores inside and outside of the house. Liza's life, up to that point, was no fairytale, which is why she often fantasized of a happily ever after kind of existence.

As the oldest, she was made to do the hardest chores, take care of the younger children in the home, and never allowed to simply be a little girl. It was not unusual for Liza to be sent outside in the cold of winter, day or night, to find wood for the stove and to then begin preparing meals for the next day when she was back in the house. Though she never uttered that she thought it was all so unfair, she has never forgotten.

On one occasion, her stepfather said that if she promised to wake before dawn to cut wood, start a fire to warm the house, and cook his breakfast for two weeks, he would buy her a fancy dress. Liza was so excited that she even did chores that were for her sisters, Leah and Beth. When it was time to get her new dress, little did she know, but Leah would get one also, without having to do one thing extra to earn it. Leah was the Butch's first born and that's another thing that has bothered Liza for years. The extra she did was supposed to be for her to have something special. So, she could feel special. Not Leah.

Thoughts of a better life always consumed Liza's mind. One thing she knew for sure was that she would never allow anything or anyone to keep her from her dreams. She would find a way out, one way or another, so she could have a life like her half-sister Nora had in the big house at the end of the lane. Once she escaped from life as it was now, to the one she so deserved, she vowed to never return, except maybe for holidays or special occasions to see her mother, siblings, and her favorite aunts and uncles.

Nora and Liza shared the same father and referred to each other as "half-sisters". But Liza never referred to the siblings, with whom she shared the same mother, as "halves". Maybe that was because they lived in the same house together, or maybe because she knew that they loved her more than she felt Nora did. Though Nora and Liza were less than two years apart in age, it was no secret that they were not very close. Liza viewed her older sister as a spoiled brat, who was doted on by everyone, especially her parents who bought her whatever she wanted, even red lipstick.

On many occasions, Liza had begged her own mama for red lipstick, but even with the money she earned working after school and during the summers, she was never allowed to buy any. The family needed every penny earned by every working member of the household. It was for this primary reason that each time Mama Gee gave birth to another child, Liza would share with her best friend, whose mother seemed to always have a baby at the same time, how disgusting it was for her mother to keep having all those children that they could not afford.   Years later, Liza would have that same sentiment regarding her own daughter, telling her how disgusting it was for her to be pregnant so soon, because she already had a baby who was just six months old.

When Rebecca called to tell her mom she was pregnant, Liza had a flashback to her own childhood, saying, "You're not going to give your child a chance to be a baby. She's going to be forced to help take care of a new baby and not be able to enjoy being a baby herself."

As awkward as that may sound, Rebecca simply shook her head and said, "She will be just fine since she will have a baby brother or sister to grow up with, unlike me!"

Rebecca's husband didn't know his mother-in-law very well at that point and thought the comment seemed rather odd and uncalled for. He didn't say much about how he felt at the time he heard it. Years later, having gotten used to the things his mother-in-law would say to her daughter, his wife, it made complete sense.

"Hello, Sister. Is everything okay?" Peter asked his sister as soon as she answered the phone.

Mama Gee made every effort to respond in her usual loving tone, but this time there was also a sense of anxiousness in her voice. "I am so glad you called so quickly. And, no, I'm afraid we do have a problem and as you know, it pains me to have to call under these circumstances. I know you are just getting on your feet, but something has come up and I do need a big favor."

Peter's response was as his sister expected, although she really hated having to ask anyone at all for help of any kind. When their mother died, she assumed the role of caregiver, nurturer and family matriarch. She was the one who everyone could go to for help. Even though she had little to offer tangibly, she always made a way to share whatever she had. Mostly, though, it was her big heart and kind spirit that she shared. She knew her husband was difficult to live with, and she always seemed to be able to provide her children with a satisfactory explanation of his behavior, reassuring them that everything would be okay once Butch calmed down.

This situation was different. Liza was now a young lady and couldn't handle the physical abuse that she had endured as a child. Mama Gee could also see something in the eyes of her oldest child this time, which indicated that one more altercation might result in something they might all live to regret.

CHAPTER SIX.... *Liza's Mother, Mama Gee*

When Mama Gee gave birth to Liza, her boyfriend and father of the baby, DJ asked for her hand in marriage. Unfortunately, Mama Gee's mother, Grandma Ida, was not fond of DJ and felt as though his family considered themselves to be in a class above most of the other residents in town. DJ was a local jock, with a promising future. He was tall and handsome and had a smile that would melt anyone fortunate enough to catch his eye. But he really only had eyes for one special girl.

Grandma Ida wouldn't let her daughter accept an offer of marriage, even though it may have been the right thing to do. DJ's parents, subsequently, offered to take baby Liza and allow her to be raised as the daughter of DJ's oldest sister who had been unable to conceive.

An appalled Ida, who kept her shotgun by her side at all times, raised the barrel to DJ and told him to leave and never show his face on her property again. Dare they think that they had a right to just take her daughter's child just because they had plenty of money and land? Mama Gee was actually hurt, and probably never healed, because she really had considered the proposal, and secretly thought of it as a chance for her to provide a better life for her daughter. Most of all, though, she was also in love with DJ. But she dared not challenge her mother's words. That was never done during those days.

DJ, equally disappointed, because he really did love Mama Gee, told his parents that Ms. Ida had run him away with a shotgun but he wanted to do right by this baby girl. He also had one other daughter, but didn't offer marriage to her mother when she was born because his feelings for her were not that strong. Though, later he would and she agreed.

After a few years of trying unsuccessfully to convince Ms. Ida to change her mind about their offer, DJ's parents put some money in an envelope and had it delivered, by courier, to Ms. Ida's home. In it was also a note that read, "This fulfills the obligation of our son as it pertains to baby Liza".

When Mama Gee later met and married a soldier from a neighboring town, DJ had only one message for him. "It's no secret that Liza is my daughter. I don't want any trouble so I will not disrespect the sanctity of your marriage by coming onto your property. I have heard about you around town so I'm just asking that you do no harm to my baby girl. From what I understand, she has your name now, but she still has my family's blood and will always have a piece of my heart. Do we have an understanding?"

The soldier nodded and replied, "I understand".

With those few words exchanged, the two shook hands and there was never another word spoken about Liza and her natural father until years later when Liza wanted to know why she couldn't have red lipstick like the girls at school, especially since one of them was her older sister.

"Peter, I'm afraid that something is going to happen to Liza if she stays here any longer. It would be nice if she could come to live with you and the others in the city. She could find work and maybe even learn how to work in an office. And she really needs to leave soon!"

Feeling that Liza was okay, but perhaps not for long since his sister provided no details beyond the urgency, Peter said that he would make arrangements on his end and that his sister should have Liza ready that next evening. He wouldn't be able to stay very long because he was employed as a butcher, an extremely competitive job that others were always lined up to take if given the opportunity. He had no time off for personal business of any kind. But he promised his sister that he would be on his way as soon as his shift ended that very next day; but would need to return back to the city right away so that he could be at work, knife in hand, first thing the following morning.

Peter arranged for Liza to move into the rooming house where he and other family members lived. Mama Gee could not thank her brother enough for his immediate response and promised to not only have Liza ready, but to also have ham sandwiches and Peter's favorite pineapple coconut cake packed up in a paper sack and ready for them to enjoy on the trip back to the big city.

As Peter drove through town on his way to the old house, he slowed in hopes of seeing one of his older brothers who was most often seen riding his bicycle up and down Main Street. Because he was so very young when they lost their mother, and was taken in so quickly by his uncle, Peter's memories of his siblings were a bit fragmented. Nevertheless, he knew who they all were and just liked to see them, even if just for a minute or two, whenever he traveled back home. Catching up with a few of his siblings was far easier than it was for some of the others, as he and Liza later discussed. One thing Peter knew for sure was that he was going to rescue his niece from the reigns of her stepfather. Liza waited patiently for her uncle to come to take her away to the big city.

Peter arrived to find that things were actually okay with Liza as far as he could see. He had no idea of the drama that had unfolded during the past few days. Liza was ready, with one small bag that contained all of her life's possessions. Her diary, a photograph of Grandma Ida, and the few pieces of clothing that she could take with her. Because there were so many children, they had to share everything, so she would have to get a job as soon as she made it to the city so that she could at least have the basic necessities.

Liza promised to send money back to Mama Gee to help out with the needs of the family, something she did for many years thereafter. Secretly, Liza hoped that Mama Gee would do her part to help the family by not having any more children. The youngest was almost three years old when she left home, which was a good indicator that her mama might just be finished.

After her marriage to Butch, Mama Gee seemed to have another child every two years. Two were actually born within the same year. Liza's logic was on point. Mama Gee did not have any more children after the ninth one was born. This may have been because her husband spent few nights at the old house with his family, and more time away working odd jobs to help make ends meet. That was the story back then, and it was disputed by no one.

CHAPTER SEVEN.... *Just Too Much*

Rebecca has struggled her entire life trying to figure out who she was and where she fit in. Having been married for slightly more than thirty years, she wonders if there will ever be a day when she doesn't have reminders of how she was treated by her mother as a child. After spending the day preparing a meal for the family, it only took one episode with her husband to take her back in time. It was something that one would think to be extremely trivial, but to Rebecca it was so major that it opened a wound that she was working very hard to conceal.

My husband was quite the spendthrift and it was not uncommon to find him going from room to room in our mini mansion style home that we had custom built when our children were in elementary school. On this particular day, I glanced up the front staircase and observed the ceiling fan in two of the rooms coming to a slow halt.

Earlier that afternoon I had gone upstairs to put on a load of laundry and the temperature on the second floor was reading seventy-five degrees. I reset the thermostat to seventy-two and turned on all of the ceiling fans upstairs so that the air could begin to circulate. Noticing that the fans had slowed, I went up and turned them back on and asked my husband to please leave

51

them be. It was then that I noticed that the thermostat had been reset to seventy-five degrees. As trivial as it seemed, I asked Eli to please leave the fans and thermostat the way I had set them. For some reason, he yelled at me and said that he hadn't touched them and didn't know what I was talking about.

Because I never back down from a fight, I yelled right back and before it was over, my feelings were hurt, but I had to suck it up so that Eli would not act out when the children arrived. Preparing Sunday dinner is a favorite for me, allowing time for the family to get together for food and fellowship before the start of another busy workweek.

I played the part, greeting our daughter and her fiancé, along with his brother and wife, sitting through dinner and conversation at the table for what seemed an eternity. Once everyone was gone, I helped to clear the table and put the food away, even asking Eli what he would like for lunch the next day. Eli was pretty serious about his meals and each seemed to be planned very carefully. Once I finished helping in the kitchen, I headed upstairs without saying another word to Eli. Normally, I would let him know that I was going up for the evening. Our daughter teases and says we act like we have a shop on the first floor, the way we "close up downstairs" before heading upstairs, where we stay for the remainder of the day.

During our more than thirty years together, we had developed a nightly routine, with Eli selecting and ironing his clothes for work the next day while I showered. But when Eli got upstairs he found me on the sofa in the sitting area of our bedroom fully clothed. He didn't say a word. He simply opened his closet door and went on as he would normally, selecting clothes for the next day, and laying them out so he wouldn't disturb me in the morning as he prepared himself for work. In the meantime, I busied myself, trying to ignore my husband as best I could, by checking my email and responding to messages I had received earlier.

Once I decided it was time to shower for bed, I did so, and still without a word spoken between the two of us. Eli knew there was something wrong and eventually asked why I was so very quiet. I responded, "no reason" because I knew in my heart that he understood why I was behaving so oddly all of a sudden, even as he chose to pretend as though he didn't have a clue. Eli was trying to take a stand and was mad at me for accusing him of something he said he didn't do, even though he knew that I assumed he had, because it was behavior that was typically characteristic of him. He was always turning off lights and adjusting the thermostat to help save on utility bills.

For what seemed forever, we sat in silence, neither wanting to be the first to give in. Eli didn't because he knew he had to get up for work at five in the morning, and I didn't because my feelings were hurt. For some reason, I felt that Eli always managed to treat me very nicely when it was just the two of us together, but whenever we were to be in the company of others, he would sometimes act differently.

He would occasionally seem to behave in a way that reminded me of my life as a child in the house with my mother. That type of flashback would always send me into a tailspin. I would have to, yet again, remind my dear husband of what I shared with him early on in our relationship: I will not be a wife like my mother; nor will be married to a man like my father. Active communication was a must for me. Anything else was a deal breaker.

Fortunately, my husband and I had a relationship that allowed us to have dialogue whenever something seemed out of sorts, making a pact to never close our eyes if we were not on one accord. It might take a few minutes for one or the other to come around, but one of us had to break the silence at some point. I can't count on one hand the number of times we have gone to sleep without working out any issue that may have come up. Well, Eli may have tried to go to sleep, but I would always make it hard for him to avoid the fact that things were not right. And if I ever get so upset that I leave the room, it is Eli who come to find me. This was something I learned from my mom's younger sister, who had the absolute perfect family life from my point of view.

One thing that everyone knew was that Eli really loved his "wife", as most heard him refer to me. He may have acted a little out of the ordinary at times, but he loved me with all of his whole heart and soul and never wanted to see me hurt by anyone. And as hard as it was for him to do he had tolerated me being mistreated, disregarded, subtly and directly for many years from the one person who should love me as much as he does. That one evening for me was obviously a pivotal one for him as well.

One day, soon after that little episode that we had, Eli finally reached capacity and the pot inside of him began to boil over. He was forced to open up and share what he had witnessed for nearly thirty years and it was not a pretty picture. And it was not well received at all. The one on the receiving end was none other than my own mother, Liza.

On our last visit to see my mother in her home, we had some very strange things to happen. Just like every other time we had visited, it ended up as a work of labor for Eli and somewhat for me since I would never rest until he did. This time, Eli had painted rooms, shampooed carpets on both levels, repaired the back porch, hung ceiling fans, not to mention the touch ups to this and that. We had planned to visit some friends but with all that my mother had for him to do, there wasn't much time, since we were only in town for three days.

The last straw this trip was on our final evening, as we were scheduled to meet friends for dinner. My mom told Eli that he still hadn't completed all that she had for him to do. Curtains were yet to be rehung. Having had enough of my husband working from sun up to sun down since we arrived at her house, I grabbed the curtains from my mother, hopped on top of her couch with my shoes on and started to hang them myself. Enough was enough.

Seeing the rage that was coming from me nonverbally, they both started to help. I paid no attention to any comments by my mother about how I was hanging her curtains the wrong way. If she didn't like it, she could fix it or have someone else to do it some other time.

For years I had been overcompensating for what my dad wouldn't do for her, and Eli had helped whatever the task, without ever complaining. But this time was a bit much. I started to realize that maybe I had been a meal ticket for her all these years and now she was using me. After the last curtain was hung, Eli and I changed our clothes, and left to go spend an hour or two with our friends. We decided not to stay out too long so that we could get back to the house to pack and rest up before leaving that next morning. Or so we thought.

When my dad passed away, my mother wanted all reminders of him gone. The last to go was the floor model television that had been in their house for decades. One of my friends said that she would take it, so that was something else that my mother wanted done before we left. As soon as we walked in from dinner, she asked when we were going to take the television to my friend. Not, how was dinner? Or, did you enjoy the little bit of time you had with your friends? I told her that my friend wasn't available until later that weekend and that they would call to make arrangements.

"Why can't you all just take it over there?", she shouted.

I told her that number one, because it was too heavy for Eli to move by himself and I didn't lift furniture anymore; and number two, because we would be leaving first thing in the morning and we had a twelve-hour drive ahead of us. All of a sudden, my mother starts cussing and fussing about how we were leaving her with that piece of crap and how sick she was of looking at it. I ignored her ranting, with no response whatsoever, so she went into her bedroom, slammed the door, and stayed closed up in there until the next morning. We heard her laughing and talking to someone on the phone, but she had no conversation for us at all.

We had both had just about enough. All she wanted from us was for me to buy her stuff, and for Eli to come to her house to do work. No real quality time at all. Just work. Conversations with me were always strained, but she would at least engage Eli, over coffee first thing in the morning before she put him to work. He later shared with me that it was almost as though she was trying to pull him into her web of resentment towards me. The way she would look at me when I appeared while they were talking was the strangest thing he had ever witnessed, but he had almost gotten used to it. She was say things like, "What does she want?" or "Uh oh, here she comes!"

Anyway, wanting morning to come sooner than later, we got all of our belongings together and sat the bags by the door of the bedroom we were in. After showering and getting into bed we started to smell an odor that was quite strange. At first thought, I assumed that it was perhaps nail polish remover that had spilled, and Eli thought it to be some type of bug spray. We got up and checked the hallway area for the odor but it was isolated and in our room only, and right by the bed. We both started to feel a little paranoid at that point. Was she trying to poison us in our sleep or something? Did she stage that performance like something out of one of the movies she had seen? She hadn't come out of her room at all.

We opened the windows in our room and turned both the ceiling fan and floor fan on the highest speed. Neither of us slept one bit. As a matter of fact, Eli called and made a reservation at a hotel across the state line, so that we could get some rest before the longest leg of our journey back to our home.

My mother was up and sitting in the kitchen having coffee before we made our way downstairs. Eli waited for me, so that attempts wouldn't be made to lure him into the kitchen for coffee. Once downstairs, we opened the front door and immediately started to load our belongings into the car. My mom appeared as we were going back into the house for the last of our things.

"Oh, Eli, I made coffee." She said without looking my direction at all.

"I'm okay. Thanks," is all he said.

To our surprise, as though she had forgotten how awful she was to us the night before, in the strangest tone we have ever heard from her, she said, "You sure you don't want to stay another night?"

Eli looked at me, I looked at him, and we didn't look at my mother at all as we continued downs the front steps to the car, pretending as though we didn't hear a word she said. Once in the car, Eli said that it would be a cold day in hell before spent another night in that house, and he was not one to say bad words. He added that he would be hard pressed to go back in there at all, if only for a minute.

"There's something really wrong with your mother. She obviously doesn't like you at all, and she treats both of us like slaves. I'm done." And that was all that either of us said until we were on the main highway headed away from the city of Belmont. Neither of us have returned since that day.

As strange as it sounds, it took this incident at my mother's house to unfold for me to stop and take closer look at myself. I finally realized that it was time for me to understand me! Who am I, and just where do I fit in to the grand scheme of the family I have always known and loved?

We had been back home for a couple of weeks when my mother called. I hadn't bothered to call to let he know that we had made it back home. She said that she had called several times and that neither of us answered the phone. I told her that we were busy with work. She and I spoke only a couple of times after that, and the conversation between the two of us was as strained as it usually was. No big deal. However, she was very concerned that Eli had not spoken to her at all, and she wanted to know why.

Eli had stated that he didn't want to talk to my mom because he could no longer hold back the things he wanted to say to her about the way she was towards me. I told him that it was fine and that if he needed to talk to her to get it out, that was understandable. I thought that would be better than having him to hold it in, like what I had done for my whole entire life.

The next time my mother called she asked, "Why doesn't Eli talk to me anymore?"

"He will have to tell you himself." I replied.

As usual, she spoke to me with that tone that was bitter and condescending all at the same time, "You're his wife, why don't you just tell me."

"Because this is between the two of you. Hold on." And with that I gave Eli the phone.

Eli takes the phone from me, "Hello."

"Hi. I just wanted to know why you don't talk to me anymore. We always had such nice conversations, but now you're so different."

"I really don't have much to say to you. On that last night at your house we were afraid for our lives, because of some fowl, odor that was concentrated in our room only."

"What! Are you trying to say that I tried to kill you and your wife?" my mother says to Eli.

"Hey, I'm only saying that we have never smelled anything like that before, and it was only in our room. And you were mad because we left before finishing the work you wanted me to do. I was tired and we didn't even get a chance to enjoy the visit as we planned. And then we get back to smell something that was so bad that we were afraid to go to sleep".

Seeming very agitated with what Eli was saying to her, my mother replies, "I can't believe this. If you were so afraid, why didn't you wake me up to ask me what it was?"

"Are you serious. We just knew we had to get out of there. Also, I need to tell you that I have watched, without saying one word, for over twenty-nine years, the way you have treated my wife. You are mean to her. You always look at her with an expression that would make anyone cringe, and you hardly have anything nice to say to her at all. You are always expecting her to do things for you, and you come here to our house and stay in your room without interacting much with her at all.

"My wife bends over backwards trying to make you happy, buying this and that for you, making the room upstairs just right for you, and you take that all for granted. Like she's supposed to do things for you.

"We know that you really come here to spend time with your brother, because you can hardly ever wait to get to his house or to talk to him on the phone. The last time you were here, you left your granddaughter's graduation party to go over to your brother's, because you didn't like all the people who were here.

"Those people, as you consider them, care about us and you should be happy. We hear you in your room laughing and talking on the phone, but with us you seem annoyed and treat us as though we have the plague or something, getting mad at us for no reason.

"You make it uncomfortable for us in our own home and in yours. You might talk to me, but if you don't have much to say to my wife, I can't just ignore that. And I'm not going to just take it anymore without letting you know how I feel."

With that, Eli was done and my mother's translation was that he said really mean and had said awful things to her.

CHAPTER EIGHT.... *Initial Epiphany*

After many years of wearing blinders and turning deaf ears to the many snide remarks, Rebecca had finally realized why she and her mother didn't have the typical relationship one would expect of a mother and daughter, especially when the daughter is an only child. She realized that she was merely an obligation. Her mother never wanted to have children, as she so openly admitted to someone near and dear to her only child, during a graduation celebration Rebecca and Eli hosted for their daughter.

It was during a conversation that some of the more seasoned guests were having about how proud they were of their children and grandchildren that Liza decided to say the unthinkable. She used that time as an opportunity to share with people she barely knew, who were there to support her granddaughter, that she never wanted to have children.

"I mean, Rebecca is my daughter, but I never wanted to have her. But I did, so here we are."

The other ladies were in total shock. "Who would say something like that?" they thought to themselves.

A few days after Liza left to travel back to her home, one of the ladies decided that Rebecca needed to know about the shocking comment made by her mother, so she called her on the phone to share the whole story. Immediately after spilling it all, Annie, who had been like a mother to Rebecca, wanted to take it all back. Almost immediately after hanging up the phone, she called back and asked Eli if he and Rebecca would come over to her house because she needed to tell her something.

Before they could get in the door good, Annie reached out to hug Rebecca as she tearfully said, "I am so sorry for telling you all of that. As soon as I hung up the phone, my husband and I both agreed that I may have been out of line and I want you to know that I am so very sorry". As Rebecca watched the tears form in her dear friend's Annie's eyes, she told her that it was okay. She explained that she has always known that she was not really wanted by her mom, so hearing this was just confirmation. She reassured Annie that she would be okay and that her sharing that bit of news was another added piece to the puzzle of her life. It had been obvious to Rebecca for years that her mother's feeling towards her was somewhere between love and despise.

Love was what she was supposed to feel as a mother, so Liza would put that face on whenever it was needed. She had watched enough movies to know how to really perform. In front of her own mother, and in front of neighbors and some friends, the show was quite convincing when Rebecca was a little girl. The older Rebecca became, the harder it was for Liza to hide the fact, that secretly she has always despised Rebecca for getting in the way of her dream.

Liza wanted the life of the elite. She wanted to live like the characters in the books she had read and in the movies that she had watched. And like the fancy women on the soap operas, with nice clothes and makeup.

Believing that she had finally met someone who had the potential to give her the good life, Liza could finally begin life anew, leaving all of the hurt from the past behind. The man who would rescue her was a cop, and his beat was in the neighborhood of the five and dime store where she was employed. Mason walked into the store, took a seat on one of the stools at the food counter, and immediately caught Liza's eye.

Not wanting to look so fresh from down south, Liza used lady like manners just like the movie stars did. She even batted her eyes, glancing in the opposite direction attempting to appear like she was someone from the right side of the tracks. Having watched so many movies, this performance was almost second nature. Liza was very pretty, with dark wavy hair that adorned her face and a body that would make any soldier turn to look two, and maybe even three times.

Mason was originally from the Midwest. He had served in the military for a short tour of duty and took up residence in the big city when his time had ended. He loved the attention he got from women when he was in uniform so he decided he would try that same type of attire on the civilian side as a police officer. He had served in what he thought to be the toughest branch of service, which made his job on the police force not as challenging as it could have been otherwise. Mason wasn't very thick and didn't weigh very much at all. But he was a tall, handsome smooth-talking man, who had travelled the country from coast to coast, which helped him to impress any lady fortunate enough to catch his eye.

For Liza, this was perfect. Meeting Mason happened at just the right time. It wasn't very long after they started to date that Liza ended up pregnant, which was a surprise for Mason. Not what he expected at all. He already had a child back home who was just an infant, and had no plans of that happening again any time soon.

Though he was no longer in a relationship with his son's mother, he had reconnected with her while he was on a short visit home before settling in the city, which is when she got pregnant. The two had dated while they were in high school, but broke up soon after Mason joined the service.

Liza wanted to get married right away because she wanted to keep her reputation as being a good girl. She didn't want the people back home to find out that she was pregnant out of wedlock and think otherwise. To Liza's dismay, it wasn't until Rebecca was seven months old that Mason finally agreed to get married. In all actuality, the only reason he agreed to get married was because Liza ended up pregnant again less than three months after Rebecca was born. She pleaded with Mason to marry her this time. There was no way she could tell Mama Gee that she was going to have yet another baby without a husband, so she and Mason went to the local courthouse to legalize their nuptials just a few months before she was to give birth to her second child.

None of this was ever to be shared with her daughter. Liza didn't want Rebecca to see her as anything other than perfect. She never willingly shared anything about her childhood with her daughter, nor did she want her to hear it from anyone else. For whatever reason, Liza was able to convince everyone to help her to keep most of the details of her life from her daughter. Everything was considered a secret and no one ever broke their promises to Liza. She had that kind of effect on people, even after they were all grown up with families of their own.

As a matter of fact, Rebecca only found out about the actual date that her parents were married because she was able to see it on the marriage license after Mason passed away. Even then, Liza tried to keep her from seeing the document. She never wanted Rebecca to know that she was born out of wedlock.

It must have been a secret that both of her parents decided to take to their graves, because Mason, who had always told Rebecca just about everything, never shared that detail. Other than this one little piece of information, Mason's life was an open book for his daughter to know whatever she wanted, and he enjoyed sharing even the most intricate of details with his little girl. He was the first to share with Rebecca that her mom had become pregnant soon after she was born, giving birth to a baby boy. Sadly, Mason also shared that her little brother, his and Liza's second and last child, had only lived for two days.

When asked the circumstances regarding her little brother, Liza would only say that she was working one day and on the way home she started to hemorrhage. By the time she made it to the hospital, she was told that the baby was coming and they were unable to stop her labor, even though it was two months before the actual delivery date. Because of complications, the baby only survived for two days. Liza said the doctors told her then that it was not very likely that she would survive another pregnancy, so she took heed and never became pregnant again.

CHAPTER NINE.... *Those Things Yet Untold*

Rebecca's earliest memories as a baby include things that happened during those times when she was left to stay at her parent's home. At the conclusion of visits with family who lived in the big city, everyone else would go back home with Mama Gee. However, given the fact that her mom's sister, Leah, and some other relatives had also relocated to the big city up north, Mama Gee said it was okay for Rebecca to stay longer. They could help take care of her during the day while Liza and Mason were both at work. One cousin reminds her each time she sees him of how he had to drag her by her ear to her mom's job, saying that he couldn't watch her anymore. He had enough of the little sweet Miss Rebecca on this one particular day.

"She's not a real baby. I'm telling you, this child has been here before. You all think she is a sweet little girl, but she is really a grown up in a little girl's body. Liza, I hope you understand that I love the family and I have tried to help, but she turns into another person as soon as she sees you step foot on that bus. I declare she waits patiently, watching you from the window, smiling and singing as she eats her cereal that we all know she is never going to finish."

I used to take so long to eat my food and would sometimes take a nap right on the table, waking up only to see the same food still there. When I could, I would feed it to my

71

best friend, Puffy, a full-bred white German Sheppard. My dad only got the best for me, and pets were no exception. Puffy was well trained and was as anxious to see me, as I was to see her when I would return for visits. If it was not Puffy waiting for me to sneak her food, it was my mom's youngest brother who would wait patiently for someone to say that I could leave the table. Having prayed for the moment for his little niece, who was just a few years his junior, he would then devour the cereal or whatever I hadn't finished. We would eat name brand food from the grocery store while in the big city, but once back home with Mama Gee, it was food from the garden and from the freezer. Food that had been canned, frozen, and then stored in either the icebox or cabinets, ready to feed the many mouths Mama Gee always had at her table.

Scratching his head as he searched for the right way to tell his cousin that he'd had enough, Jeff continued, "But today, Liza, all I told her was to finish her cereal and she took that spoon and looked me dead in the eye and threw it and hit me right smack in the center of my forehead. I never told you that she had done this before, but this time it was so hard that I felt like I was seeing stars. Mama Gee said we are not to touch her, so I didn't lay a hand on her. But I 'clare, I can't continue to be abused by a three-year old"!

Cousin Jeff left the store shaking his head as I smiled at the ladies sitting at the counter drinking their coffee, pretending as though I had no clue what he was talking about.

Without having many options at the time, the only thing my mom could think to do was to take me to her sister Leah's house. This sister had just had her first baby so the last thing my mom wanted to do was burden her with the added stress of caring for me. But she called ahead and Leah told her that it would be fine. My mom had to get back to work so Leah was waiting at the door when we arrived.

It was time for her to feed the baby so my aunt told me to go into the room where the baby was and to watch him while she fixed his bottle. To her dismay, she came back in the bedroom moments later to find her baby being dangled on the side of the bed, by none other than her sweet and precious niece. Me! Aunt Leah called Mama Gee and told her what I had done and also about the incident with cousin Jeff. Mama Gee did then what she continued to do all of my life, she came for me. Didn't they know that was all I wanted anyway? I missed Mama Gee and was excited when she arrived that Saturday to take me back home.

Later that year I did go back for another visit. I hadn't been there more than a few days, and it became obvious that I needed more attention than provided by my parents. I was

73

never alone when at Mama Gee's house. There was always someone around and Mama Gee never took her eyes off of me. If she left the room, I was usually right on her trail. Other times, I was playing with the other children or cared for by my mom's other sister who was a teenager and still living at home. Not used to me being around, it wasn't unusual for me to wander off before it was noticed by either parent. Mostly my mom, as my dad was hardly ever around.

On this one occasion, while my mom was busy in another part of the house, I decided that I wanted to shave like I had watched my grandfather and dad do. So, I went into the bathroom, climbed up on the toilet, slid onto the sink, reached up and opened the cabinet door. It was called a medicine cabinet, but all kinds of interesting things were in there. A jar of ointment, a tube of toothpaste, some other things that I had never seen before, and then there it was. That razor blade I would see my dad using.

My turn, I thought to myself. It was folded in half and as I tried to open it up, before I knew it, I had sliced my pointer finger and started to bleed. I screamed and my mother came running. She immediately started to scold me and yelled, "what are you doing in here anyway?"

After wrapping my finger with a cloth, we headed right away to the hospital emergency room which was fortunately in walking distance from the house. Because there was blood and since I was such a cute little girl, it didn't take long for me to be seen.

When the doctors unwrapped the cloth to look at my finger, they looked at me and asked what happened. Pointing with the other hand in the direction of my mom, I whimpered and said, "She tried to cut my finger off"! My mother immediately began to explain what really happened, as they repaired and bandaged my wound. They must have believed her because there was never another question or mention of my version of the incident again.

Since cousin Jeff would no longer help babysit, and my mom and dad both had to work, it was my aunt Leah, the same aunt whose son I nearly dropped on his head, who said "Bring her to me and we will work it out."

By this time the baby was older, and knew when to cry when something was wrong. Also, my aunt's husband, Roy, would be at home and available during most days now because he only worked odd jobs and they were few and far between. So, I would be left at home with him whenever my aunt was away.

It wasn't until I was in my early thirties did I tell my mother why I refused to let my children spend a night with their cousins at my aunt's house. I told her that the times when

75

I had to stay over my aunt's house, almost as soon as she or my aunt were out of the door, and clear from sight, Roy would lay the baby down in the other room and ask me if I wanted to watch television. Of course, I would say yes; and he would sit with me on the couch and cover the two of us with a blanket.

With his legs sprawled, he would take my tiny hand and put it on his penis, telling me how nice that felt to him, that it was our secret, and that if I told anyone about it that Mama Gee would get very upset and wouldn't come back to pick me up. And he also told me that I would be the one to get into trouble because I wasn't supposed to be watching television. I was young and didn't know any better. The only thing I knew was that I wanted to go home to my Grammi's house and whatever I had to do or not do to make that happen is what would be. I don't recall him ever doing anything more than that, though that was enough. I never said a word.

Later, when I was older but not yet a teenager, my aunt's two sons, who were each three and five years younger than me, respectively, were encouraged by their dad, this same man, to try to touch me on my breasts and on my private spot at night when we went to bed. The reason I was at their house was because we were waiting for Mama Gee to come for us.

By the time I was ten years old, I didn't have to wait for Mama Gee to come for me. I was allowed to travel on the bus or airplane by myself, and for some reason I would always have to stop over at my aunt's instead of going straight to Waters Edge.

We all had to sleep together in the same bed, which was not uncommon in those days, and her husband seemed to always be the one left with us during the night. I recall beating my young cousins off of me each time they tried to make a move.

When I screamed, their father would just open the door ever so slightly and say, "Y'all need to stop all that noise", with a snicker and sly grin, which let me know that he knew exactly what they were up to.

But not with me they wouldn't! I didn't tell their mom or Mama Gee because I didn't want them to get a real beating. I was able to handle them myself so I never said a word.

Eventually, they got tired of the beatings I would give them and they stopped trying to bother me. I don't know what their dad said about it, and I didn't care. I was ready for him too. Each time I had to stay over with them, and especially if Roy was there, I would sleep with one eye open, sheets tucked around me as tightly as possible, with a huge rock in my hand, ready to punch him in the nose if he dared try to touch me himself.

I was no joke when it came to fighting. My mother's stepfather taught me how to defend myself from boys, since I was the only girl in the house with Mama Gee after my mom's youngest sister, who I called Sissy, married and moved away. No one in my mom's family played when it came to doing anything to hurt me and I knew that.

I pretty much felt that my cousins were only doing what their dad told them, and since I was never hurt by any of it, and handled it with them myself. It was fine. I failed to mention that though he was indeed married to my aunt, I have never referred to him as my uncle, for obvious reasons.

In response to what I shared about what happened with Roy and the boys, my mom simply said one thing to me. "Don't you ever mention any of this to your daddy. You know what he will do". Yes, I knew. He would have driven the four hundred plus miles from his house to where Roy lived, and killed him dead! But for my mom, she must have been thinking about the life she wanted to keep for herself, and possibly what others would think about her putting me in a situation for something like that to happen.

Not, "Oh, sweetie, I am so sorry this all happened to you and I wish you had told me sooner". Nothing like that at all.

I never spoke of it again. But interestingly enough, from that point on, my mom thought it was okay to call to tell me of little things that she thought was cute that her brother-in-law did, or each occasion that he was sick and in the hospital. She even had the nerve to lead her sister to believe it was okay to ask me to be on the program for his funeral when he passed away. And when I declined, it was as though I had done the unthinkable and was no longer there for the family!

Why didn't my mom speak up for me and say to her sister that it wouldn't be a good idea for me to be included? My dad was already deceased, just like Roy! My dad, Mason, had passed away just over three years prior. I've not been able to figure out the reason my mom chose not to stand up for me, especially for something as awful as that? I didn't quite get it then, though later it would all become very clear.

CHAPTER TEN.... *Adolescent Woes*

As a little girl in the town where Rebecca lived with her parents, everyone always treated her special. There were a few neighbors who were older, who never had children so they would have a special treat for her on holidays and special occasions. Other children would knock on their doors for a treat, but they only answered for Rebecca. As such, there were plenty of extra eyes to look out for Rebecca anytime she was left home alone. There was a family nearby whose house she loved visit. With five children, two girls and three boys, all near the same age, it was like being down home at Mama Gee's. Every once in a while, the two teenagers were often tasked with looking out for the younger siblings, and when Rebecca would visit, she would be included.

Everything was great until that awful day that I was violated by the teenage boy while the others, including the oldest sister, watched in disbelief from across the room. He ruined everything for me. Being with them gave me what I longed for the most. Life with brothers and sisters. During one of the nights I slept over, he came into the room and asked his little sister and me if we were doing something that we shouldn't have been doing. I was half asleep when I heard him, and then the unthinkable happened. He yelled something terrible about

80

being nasty as he yanked the covers off of me and pulled down my pajama pants, but not my panties.

I was horrified. He touched me inappropriately and said he needed to check for himself. The older sister watched as he rubbed my private parts like one would rub a splintered piece of wood with sandpaper. It hurt terribly and I screamed and kicked for him to leave me alone, but neither sister nor the other brothers said a word. It ended after what seemed to last forever, but was really only seconds.

When he finished, he sniffed his fingers and said to the older sister, "I don't know what all that noise was up here, but I guess they were telling the truth".

Although there was no penetration, I will never forget how violated I felt. He told me that I had better not tell or he would do it again and make it hurt for real the next time. I wasn't even ten years old.

I didn't go back to sleep that night, and just like with my cousins and their dad, I kept the covers tucked around me as tightly as I could. I didn't have my rock with me, otherwise this situation would have had a much different outcome.

At the first sight of dawn, I got out of bed before any of the other children, ran downstairs and asked their mom if I could go home. I didn't even take the time to brush my teeth or wash my face. I wanted to get out of there as fast as I could. As

I ran, what seemed like forever to get home, I wondered what I had done to make him do that to me. I never told, because I really was afraid of him, and I also knew that my dad would kill him if he ever found out. He would kill anyone who hurt me, a promise he kept and one I believed until the day he left this earth.

I never asked to spend the night with that family again. Anytime my mom needed to go somewhere, I pleaded with her to let me stay home. Not comfortable leaving me home alone at night, she asked another neighbor's teenage daughter to come over to sit with me. She was always excited to earn a dollar or two. Her boyfriend would wait until the coast was clear and he would come over too. When her company arrived, I was told to go to bed so they could have privacy. I would do just that. But I didn't dare close my eyes. I kept my clothes on under my pajamas, tucked the covers around me as tightly as I could, and kept a rock in each of my hands just in case anyone dared to mess with me again. I never said a word.

Oh, I forgot to mention where I learned to keep a rock with me for defense. My dad had two sisters, with an age difference of nearly twenty years his junior. The eldest of the two, Cindy, was only six years older than me. Cindy loved to talk about how excited she was when she found out that I had been born. Because of me, she was made an auntie when she was only six years old. And she took her role as "auntie" very seriously, always reminding me to let her know if anyone ever bothered me.

She told me that I had to make sure that I never appeared to be afraid of anybody, and to always keep a rock or two in my coat pockets. She took the time to show me how to ball up my fist with the rock inside without anyone ever knowing. She told me that it would pack a powerful punch and even break someone's nose. I didn't want to go that far, but I promised her that I would do whatever was necessary to let people know that I was not the one to pick on.

Growing up in the projects, my dad had to be tough to survive, and he had quite the reputation, even as an adult. He was an all-city athlete, spent a few years in the military, served on the police force in the big city, all of which added to the reputation he had earned as being a no nonsense kind of guy. He didn't want me to be a bully or anything like that, simply for me to be able to handle myself if ever needed. To be sure, he insisted that I stay in the karate classes until he was comfortable that I could really defend myself, both physically and mentally.

Too bad I didn't have that training a few months sooner. I would have been able to keep that boy from hurting me the way he did. I wouldn't have hurt my little cousins, but I sure would have taken those rocks to the big city to punch that awful Roy in his nose as hard as I could.

My training was really only put to use one time, and that was to fight a girl who passed a note in our seventh-grade homeroom class saying that she was going to beat me up after school. Everyone knew what that meant, so crowds began to form and walk in the same direction that I walked home from school. Because I didn't want to get in trouble for fighting, I deliberately walked right past my house and around the corner before stopping to wait for the girl to get there with her entourage. As fights would go back then, a circle formed around us, and closed in pushing us closer and closer together. I took deep breaths, as I had learned in my karate classes, and gripped my hands tightly around those rocks as I had learned from my auntie.

Before I knew it, I had closed my eyes, pulling both hands out of my pockets as someone yanked my coat off of me like I was a master fighter in a ring. We both started to swing but it was me who landed the first and only punch, hitting the girl directly in her nose.

I remembered hearing her sister yell, "I'm gonna get you now. You broke my sisters nose."

Fortunately, before a major riot erupted I heard a voice saying, "Break it up, break it up now."

Mr. Mann, who just so happened to be the grandfather of the children who lived two houses down from where we lived, immediately stopped his car when he saw the commotion. It was safe to do that back then, as children had major respect and fear of any grown up. The village was in full effect.

As he pushed his way through, and eventually reached the inside of the crowd of now overly excited children, with a surprised look and even more surprised tone, Mr. Mann shouted, "REBECCA, is that you? Now you know that you know better. I did not expect to find you anywhere near here and definitely not one of the ones fighting. And it seems you hurt that little girl pretty bad. I hope you didn't start it, but either way I'm gonna have to tell your mother on you".

At that moment, I cringed because that meant that Mama Gee would find out that I had been involved in a fight. And the last thing I ever wanted to do was to disappoint my grandmother.

Mr. Mann told all of the children "Get away now, and you all better go straight home."

He took his belt off to signal that he was indeed serious. Everyone scattered for fear that he would beat each child on the spot, and follow that up with a phone call to parents, which was the expected and likely thing to do during those days.

Rather than allow me to walk, and possibly continue the fight, he took me by my arm and put me in the back seat of his station wagon, and drove me around the corner to my house. As the car pulled up to the curb in front of my house, I saw the front door open, which meant my dad was home. Before he could say another word, I jumped out of the car saying that my mother wasn't home yet, and ran up the front steps two at a time, hurrying to get away from the chastising I had received from Mr. Mann, who also happened to be a minister. Now I was also going to be in trouble with God. Oh no!

Although my dad was home when we got there, I didn't expect Mr. Mann to get out of the car to go in to speak to him about the fight. Most people were kind of afraid to say much of anything to him, especially if it had anything to do with me, because he would cuss them out, threaten to beat them up, or worse.

He would likely have said, "You better get out of here with that nonsense about my little girl before I knock you slam out." My dad didn't make many idle threats either, so Mr. Mann didn't even bother to get out of the car to walk with me to the door; but he did promise to have his daughter to call my mother right away to tell her everything.

When I walked into the house with my coat in my hand, my dad calmly asked what happened. His easy chair was positioned right by the door so it was rare for anything or anyone to go by the house, walking or driving, without him knowing. From the corner of his eye, he had watched as I got out of Mr. Mann's car, and knew that it had to be for a reason. As soon as I walked in the door I began to explain myself telling him that a girl threatened me and I had to fight her.

To that my dad's response was very matter of fact, "Did you win?"

Rubbing my hands together, I said, "I think so. There was blood on her face after I punched her in the nose with my fist."

All my dad said in response was, "Okay, that's all I want to know. You don't seem to be hurt so I don't have to go check nobody. Go on upstairs now and get changed before your mother gets home. You have blood on your top and your hair is all over your head, and you know she will have a fit if she sees you looking like that."

By the time my mom got home, I had washed my top by hand to get the blood out that had obviously splattered from that one punch, or maybe two. My mom called me downstairs and asked why my top was hanging on the clothes line in the basement. Before I could respond, she told me not to even think about telling a lie because she knew everything. She told me how embarrassing it was for her to have the neighbor to call her on her job to tell her that someone had to break up a fight that I was in the middle of.

"What do you think the neighbors are going to say about that, Rebecca. You should be ashamed of yourself! They will say I'm a bad mother to have a child acting like a heathen in the street, fighting like some commoner".

I tried to explain what happened, but being from the south where ladies didn't behave like that, she had little empathy for me. And she never once asked if I was hurt. I later heard her talking on the phone, telling the whole story and laughing about me acting like I was a champion fighter. She also told whomever she was talking to that I had obviously won the fight because I didn't have any bruises from what she could see. Though she didn't let on to me, I do believe she was actually very proud of me.

Many years later, my mother was talking about the neighbors and told me that the mean boy, as everyone in the neighborhood referred to him as, had actually grown into a fine young man. He had gotten married, and had relocated to another state. She often told me that during his visits home, he would always ask about me. I asked that she not share my contact information with him, but never told her the reason. All I know is that the timid little girl that he once violated is now a full-grown woman; and that mean little boy who was also a molester, will never be a fine young man in my eyes. And if I see him again, he just might be reminded of that awful day.

The best part about the neighborhood, though, was the lady next door and her husband. The Jacobs. Most people thought we were related because we ended up being as close family. To my knowledge, the assumption that we were family was never denied by any of us. When my grandmother first met Mr. and Mrs. Jacobs, she thanked them for looking out for us because my mother and I were so far away from home.

Grammi said she felt that God had placed us next door to them, and she thanked Him for that in her prayers every night. When she would come for me at the end of each school year, the two of them would sit in the backyard for hours as the sun set, sipping on nothing but a glass of ice water or a cold pop, discussing life from each of their perspectives. They were both born in the south during the same era, and though separated by several states, they had much in common.

They each had a sincere love for their families and the Lord, and possessed the kind of spirit that made it easy for one to feel the warmth that exuberated from their hearts. I was happy that my Mama Gee connected so well with Mrs. Jacobs. Though she was caring in nature, her nieces, who visited often and sometimes stayed for long periods of time, thought she was a little too stern most of the time, but they still loved her dearly.

A feeling I echoed. I remember hearing her call my name early in the morning on weekends, like an early morning call of the rooster.

"Rebecca". "Rebecca Mae". "Rebecca". "Rebecca Mae-oo! You up? It's time to get up out of that bed now!" She would do this almost every Saturday morning.

As soon as I would hear her, I would run downstairs and open the back door that led from the house to the enclosed back porch area, opening the curtain of the window facing her yard so she could see my face.

I would just say "Good morning" and she would say, "How-do", followed by any instructions for the day that my mother had shared with her for me that she thought I needed to be reminded of.

She knew I was home alone, with my mom at work and my dad either at work or still out in the streets from the night before. On Friday's, he would get his check cashed, leave bill money for my mom on the mantle over the fireplace, and money for me on the table by the door, under an ashtray. Usually, he would return either late Sunday evening or maybe early Monday, if he had the midnight shift that week.

I got used to not seeing my dad on weekends and my mom's less than desirable attitude directed towards me the entire time. I'm sure she was embarrassed that he stayed out at night so often, as she cared a lot about what the neighbors thought. I was immune to her moods and her attitude with me. I was used to it. Used to being the target of her frustration. It was never physical, though. Only emotional and slightly verbal with the "tone" used, not the words. That's how I learned the difference between it being "how" things are said, and not only "what" is said.

My dad was always kind to me, but he and my mom fought a lot. Most of the exchanges were verbal, but occasionally there were physical altercations. Exposed to that kind of dysfunction as a child, made me vow to myself to never, ever, have a relationship like the one my parents had. How could she stand to let him treat her that way?

Well, I should know the answer to that question, because time and time again my mother reminded me that she stayed with my dad only because of me. I knew she was miserable and I always begged her to leave him, just like I begged for a brother or sister, but my yearning was always in vain. One thing I can say for sure, though, is that I was very well taken care of. I always got whatever I wanted.

Whether it was my birthday, Christmas, or just because. My dad always lived up to his promise of making sure I never went without anything I needed or wanted. Sometimes, late at night when he would come home from his nights on the town, he would come upstairs to my bedroom and kneel by my bed. I would hear him coming up the steps and would cover my head to hide. Never because I was afraid that he would try to do anything to hurt or violate me.

Sometimes though, I would cover my nose because he would smell like alcohol and I didn't like that. But I always knew that he was going to say what he always said.

"Hey little girl, are you awake?"

Eventually, I would uncover my face and giggle. It was our little game.

He would tell me how much he loved me.

"You know that you will always be my little girl and I will always give you whatever you want!"

And he would add that, "If anyone ever hurts you, I will kill them!"

I believed my dad, so I grew up confident that there was nothing I would ever want for and I always felt safe.

My mother would sometimes ask, "What did your daddy say to you?"

And I would always reply "Nothing!" I never knew why that was so important to her until much later in life.

CHAPTER ELEVEN.... *My Dad, Mason*

One thing that was for sure was that Mason loved his baby girl from the time he laid eyes on her, until the day he knew he journey was coming to an end. He only wanted what was best for her and he would move any mountain and do his best to fix any situation that got in the way of anything she ever wanted. This was a fact that was known to any and everyone who knew Mason, Rebecca and Liza.

I can only recall three real disagreements that I had with my dad, if they could even be called that. Once, I was admitted to the hospital for testing because my skin was very sensitive and the doctors didn't know why. When my dad came to my hospital room to visit me, I played the same game we played at home. Only this time I went a little too far and hurt his feelings.

As my dad walked through the door of my hospital room, I didn't just cover my head, this time I screamed and said, "Go away, you're a monster!"

The nurse came running when she heard my squealing, "Is everything okay."

"Yes, everything is okay, I'm her father".

"No, he's not, he's a mean old monster"! I was only seven or eight years old, but I recall that particular day now just like it was yesterday.

93

As his facial expression changed to one of hurt and disappointment, my dad turned away from me and walked out of the room.

My mother came over to check on me when she got off from work, but before asking how I felt and how I rested through the night, she immediately asked, "What did you do? What did you say to your daddy?"

"Nothing". I said with a pitiful look on my face.

She scorned at me and said, "You're a liar, what did you say?" as I cried quietly professing that I was only playing and really didn't mean what I said.

My mother just looked at me and rolled her eyes and appeared to be extremely disgusted with me. "You know what, Rebecca, if you're not more careful, you're going to ruin everything!"

I had no clue what she was talking about and I don't recall very much after that, other than the fact that my feelings were also hurt. Didn't she care that I was in the hospital and, no doubt, a little bit scared? My dad never treated me any different once I got home, so I guess he got over it.

The second incident with my dad was later that same year. I used to run from upstairs, down the steps, and hop over the ottoman, or stool as we used to call it, that sat directly in front of his recliner. It was my regular thing to do. My dad stayed in the living room, sitting in his easy chair or lying on the sofa during most of the time he spent at home. And he would always have the front door propped wide open so he could see who was coming. His easy chair was positioned directly in front of the door.

My mother hated when he would open the door first thing in the morning, keeping it open and unlocked until well after midnight. He said he didn't want to have to get up out of his chair if anyone came to the door. He thought nothing of falling asleep with the big door open and the screen door unlocked. He wasn't afraid of anyone or anything, a characteristic he passed on to me. If anyone stepped on that front porch, though, he would open one eye.

By the time I was a teenager, if one of my friends rang the bell, he would just point towards the staircase and they knew that meant for them to go on upstairs to my room. My mom hated that, as well. She didn't like anyone in her house at all, and especially not upstairs. When I started to drive, dad would be in the same spot, in his recliner with the door unlocked until I returned home from wherever.

Back then the neighborhood was relatively safe. My mom mostly hated it because of the way it looked. She always cared what others thought but my dad, being the type of person he was, didn't care at all. Another characteristic I pretty much inherited from him. He used to say that my mom "put on" for certain people and that she was "phony". He would tell me that he would never be that way and that I shouldn't be that way either. It was important for him to tell me on a regular basis that I didn't have to make people like me, and not to put up with people who thought they were "all that". That's why he made sure that I always had whatever I wanted, whenever I wanted it, so that I wouldn't have to feel inadequate or insecure. And it worked.

Anyway, that one day as I jumped over the stool, I accidentally kicked the big orange ashtray that was positioned right in the middle holding all of his keys and pocket change. This one particular time, my usual jump was off slightly, but my kick was so strong that I kicked the ashtray and it went sailing across the room, barely missing the screen of the television.

One thing everyone knew about Mason, was that second to me, he loved his jazz, his television, and his liquor (in no certain order). Which meant that the fact that I almost broke his television was a pretty big deal. He jumped up and grabbed my arm and pulled off his belt and began to whip me. I screamed and my mother came running. He only hit me two or three times but it seemed like it was two or three hundred times. He had never disciplined me before that day and my feelings were hurt more than the strikes he delivered with his belt. I'm not convinced that he wanted to hurt me. He reacted to what I did, and then had to follow through.

My mom added insult to injury by scolding me verbally, reminding me that she had told me repeatedly about running through the house. Angry with them both, I ran to my room and slammed the door, and didn't speak to either of them for days. I would leave my room only when necessary and wouldn't utter one word to either of them.

My dad went out, as usual that Friday after work. When he returned home on that Sunday night, he came to my bedside, as usual, and apologized to me. He told me that he never meant to hurt me and would never do that again. He asked me what I wanted. I said a red record player. A few days later, my new red record player was in my room when I got home from school. My mom was not happy because she felt he was letting me have my way. He didn't care how she felt. No one told him what to do. Never! Just me!

The last situation with my dad was the one that hurt me the most, and my dad also, as I later realized. That one crazy morning would prove to change the course of my life in more ways than I could ever have imagined.

One of the main things that my dad tried desperately to instill in me was the importance of education. He knew that I had potential and wanted me to perform accordingly. He never supported any of my interests outside of academics. He tried to encourage me to run track, but that never materialized, mostly because I wasn't interested. His disappointment was very obvious.

I joined the track team because he wanted me to, and one of his close friends had a daughter who was also named Rebecca and she ran track. She ended up getting a scholarship to college and for some reason my dad wanted me to follow in her footsteps, even attend the same college. What I really wanted was to be a cheerleader, but he said no because that was not for smart girls.

To appease my dad, I practiced with the track team after school, and even took a picture for the yearbook, but that was about it. I did get a chance to run in a race one time during my sophomore year of high school. He was beside himself about having the chance to finally see his little girt follow in his footsteps, and told his friends so they could as well. I wasn't excited.

I was kind of deflated from the onset of my short time on the track team, because rather than buying me the tracksuit in the same red and blue school colors as the rest of the team, my dad decided he wanted me to be different and stand out. He came home one day with a white sweat suit with red and blue stripes down the side of the pant legs and around the bands on the jacket. When I got to the field, everyone looked at me like I was from another planet, the same one I, myself, felt like I was on!

Anyway, I was so embarrassed that once it was time for me to run in the race I had been assigned, I faked a leg cramp as soon as I came out of the blocks. I immediately looked up into the stands, but rather than coming to see if I was okay, my dad and his buddies stood up with disappointment and left.

When I got home, all he said to me was, "I thought you could run!"

I reminded dad, who was an all-state track superstar in his day, that sports were his thing and that I never wanted to run anyway. I also added that I didn't like that track suit either. We never spoke of me running track again.

Too late in the school year for me to try out to be a cheerleader; and since the high school decided to have a pom-pom squad, I immediately tried out for that and was selected. I was one of only a few girls in my grade level to make it so I was extremely excited. Our squad performed at all of the home basketball games. Neither of my parents ever came to see me perform.

Fast forward now to that incident which changed my life. Forever. Or so I thought. It all had to do with a report card.

As usual, my dad came home on a Sunday after being out all weekend. This time it was in late the afternoon so I was sitting in the kitchen with my mom. That's the area of the house where she stayed most of the time. She would get up in the morning, go downstairs, take her place at the kitchen table, drink her coffee and read the local newspaper. Always so very careful, one she finished, to put the paper back together so it would be in perfect order for my dad whenever he decided to return home. After sitting at the table for a while, she would go back upstairs to take a bath, get dressed and return back to her spot at the kitchen table.

I never understood why the kitchen became her preferred place in the house. On the days that she worked, as soon as she got home, she would head upstairs to change out of her work clothes, and immediately retreat to her comfort zone. She would talk on the phone, entertain her friends, comb my hair, read her book, watch television, or just have a cup of coffee, a cold pop, or cigarette, right there in her kitchen! I imagine that not much has changed.

Anyway, when my dad arrived home that afternoon and entered through the basement door, my mom and I glanced at one another as though we knew that something was wrong. He always used the front door. This time, though, he yelled for my mom's assistance, and she quickly rushed to see what was wrong. His ankle was bleeding and he needed her to help bandage it to keep from messing up the floors inside of the house. That's her story.

I don't believe he actually thought twice about those floors. He just wanted help. I never found out for sure what really happened. I had an awesome imagination so I came up with my own theory. I told my friends that he got shot in a fight. That seemed a cool thing to have happened. My mom's version was that he hurt his leg on the door as he was getting out of the car.

She became excellent at keeping things from me, or shielding me as she would call it. Because of her pride, she didn't want the neighbors or Mama Gee or the other members of her family to think anything bad about her life, and she knew I would tell. I knew my dad would tell me what really happened to him at some point since he would tell me anything I wanted to know and then some.

This time, however, a turn of events kept that incident from coming up ever again. Once his wound was all bandaged, he went upstairs to the bathroom to get himself cleaned up from the weekend. Unlike his usual behavior, when he got back downstairs, he didn't stop at his recliner this time. He made his way back into the kitchen.

Holding a piece of paper in his hand that I didn't readily recognize, he began to question the math grade that I received for the school year's most recent quarter. I told him that I didn't know what that grade was because I hadn't yet received my latest report card.

Unexpectedly, he held up the piece of paper he had in his hand, and with a tone much more direct than he had ever used towards me, he said, "I found this in your drawer and you did not bring that math grade up like I told you".

I first asked why he was in my room going through my things. I was fifteen years old, and everyone knows how private and sensitive teenage girls were, or so I thought. Since it didn't appear as though he cared much about my feelings, I tried to explain to him that the report card he had in his hand was an old one.

For some reason, my dad's behavior seemed to become erratic as he didn't want to hear anything from me about it at all. He started yelling at me. Telling me that I was acting like a dummy. I yelled back. Pretty much screaming as loudly as I could, trying to explain to him the reason that I didn't have my current report card.

"I don't want to hear any of that nonsense", was the last thing I remember hearing him say.

And then, as if my life flashed before my eyes, my dad grabbed me by one arm and slapped me, knocking me to the floor. I screamed. My mom stood there first with her hands over her mouth, looking with disbelief. Then she started screaming at me to just stop being rebellious and give him what he wants so he would leave me alone. Instead of doing that, still screaming as loudly as I could, I jumped up, lunged towards my dad and jumped up to his level and punched him in the face. I didn't have time to think about how to use the karate I'd learned, nor did I have time to find a rock. I just fought the best I could. As expected, I was no match for him.

Because I was so confused, hurt, and angry all at the same time, I decided to give him a taste of his own medicine so I kicked his leg as hard as I could on the area that was wounded and yelled, "You're crazy. I hate you. You can't hurt me."

It was at that very moment that he grabbed my arm, digging his long, perfectly manicured fingernails deep into my skin, flinging me so hard that I went from where we were fighting in the kitchen, through the dining room, and into the living room. I stopped inches short of hitting my head on the edge of the rectangular wooden coffee table that was positioned nicely in front of the sofa.

Giving no thought to the fact that I would never win the fight with my dad, I jumped up like a cat with nine lives, and charged at him again, this time screaming "You are not going to beat me like you do those bitches and whores on the street!"

No doubt frightened by the image of a near fatal blow, my dad shook his head as he turned and walked away. Rather than continuing to taunt him with my assumptions of how he treated women on the street, I turned around and ran upstairs, slamming my bedroom door as hard as I could. It was at that point that I started to cry.

I found a way to take the doorknob off of my bedroom door so neither my mom nor my dad could get into my room even if they tried. True to what was to be expected, I picked up the phone and called my grandmother first, following that up with calls to aunts, uncles, and anyone else I thought of. I had my own phone line in my room, because that's what I wanted, so I didn't have to worry about anyone stopping me.

It wasn't long before my mother started knocking on my door, telling me to "Open the door now!"

Once I was ready, I did as she requested and opened the door. The first thing she asked was if I had called Mama Gee.

"Yes, and I told her what happened and that I am going to run away." I continued, telling my mother that she could stay with her husband if she wanted to, but I was leaving. I told her that I was not going to live there and take abuse from him like those whores on the street.

Before I knew what had happened, my mom hauled off and slapped my face, telling me how ungrateful I was, and that I had no idea what I had done by calling my grandmother and the rest of the family. I told her that she couldn't hurt me by slapping me and I was still leaving.

By that weekend, my grandmother and all of my mother's siblings and their families, even the ones who were married with children, as well as a few other family members, had driven across several state lines to where we lived. Trying to come up with a logical explanation as to why her family came to visit all of a sudden, my mother told her friends and our neighbors that our family was in town for a family reunion that she was hosting at her house. That has been the story ever since that day. Even in the conversations she and I have had about one thing or another, an acknowledgement of the real reason for the visit on such short notice has never been discussed.

The family stayed only for the weekend. Since it was an unplanned trip and they still had to work, they packed up early Sunday morning to head back home. However, my mother's youngest sister, Beth, and her husband, along with their children stayed behind.

This was the one I called "Sissy". We were very close and her husband loved me as if I were his own flesh and blood, until the day he died. And to the dismay of some others, even after having a situation to threaten our relationship many years later, he still loved me dearly. It was mutual. I always felt safe around him.

He wasn't like Roy. This particular uncle would have broken both of Roy's arms completely off, if I had told him what he did to me when I was a little girl. Unlike Roy, Uncle Al had always protected me. My earliest memory of Uncle Al was when he and Sissy were first dating. I couldn't have been much older than two or three years old. He would come over to the house and sit in the parlor to visit, which was really called "courting" back then. Mama Gee would make sure that the little children gave them their privacy. Everyone but me, of course.

On this one particular hot afternoon, mosquitos were buzzing all around. I didn't have very much hair on my head, so it was easy to spot the big fat mosquito that had nearly landed right on top of my head. Uncle Al swatted that mosquito so quick that I never even knew what happened. He was a man of few words, but he said enough that day to let me know that he wouldn't let anything or anyone hurt me.

Mama Gee had told him that she had to go on home with the rest of them family but they were to stay behind to let me gather up my things, and they were not leave that house

106

without me. As much as he loved me, he also loved Mama Gee, which meant he was going to do exactly as she said.

Hoping to change my mind, my mother came to my room and told me that she had packed my dad's suitcase and that he was going to leave. I told her that she didn't have to do that because he was her husband and she obviously wanted to stay with him. She said again, that she had only stayed with him all of those years because of me. Because she wanted me to have things in life that she couldn't give me on her own, and that she wanted me to be able to go off to school (college) when it was time, but she needed him to help make that happen.

That may have been true, but knowing my mother and how prideful she was, it was also the fact that the neighbors would want to know why I had moved away so suddenly. What on earth was she to tell them? Feeling no emotion and no regrets for the decision I made to share that awful experience with the family, I told my mother that I had made up my mind, would be fine, and would be leaving with the family that next morning. And I did.

CHAPTER TWELVE.... *The Journey Continues*

Rebecca's suitcase was packed and she was ready to go. She didn't sleep at all on the night before they were to leave. She didn't say much to her mom, who also had the light on in her bedroom most of the night. At daybreak, Beth got the children up and dressed and everyone started saying their goodbyes. Rebecca didn't think twice about her decision. She was happy knowing that she was going to be near Mama Gee again real soon and her life would be back to normal.

My dad wasn't there when we left and my mom stood in the door wiping tears from her eyes as we drove away. Not a tear formed in my eyes. I waved, excited to be heading home to live with my sissy and her family. Or so I thought. But little did I know, the oldest of the five brothers had other plans. He and his wife had a five-year old daughter, who was entering kindergarten, and a newborn baby boy. Rather than staying where I wanted, the family decided that I should go live with the brother and help him and his wife to care for their children.

His wife, Eva, worked from three in the afternoon until midnight, and Jax was a teacher during the day and attended college in the evenings, working to complete his master's degree. He was the smart one in family, and was able to plead his case with the family, that I would be better off with him, since he had the academic training to ensure that I stay focused on my studies. He was quite convincing, a skill that later in life ended up being to my detriment, as far as the family was concerned. My mother was all for me moving in with him, not necessarily because it was best for me, but mostly because she didn't want me to move in with her sister.

Although she loved her youngest sister my mom didn't approve of the life style she lived. And her husband had a younger brother that my mom felt they were trying to fix me up with. My mom later admitted to me that she didn't want me there because she didn't want me to end up like Beth, who had married into a very religious family. They were extreme in their beliefs and it sometimes made my mom and many of their other siblings uncomfortable to be around them.

Sissy didn't dress like the other women in the family. She wasn't allowed to wear pants, makeup or fancy hairstyles; something my mom didn't think was good for me to be around. I never told anyone about my mom's opinion of her sister, Beth's, life. And even though I did have quite the liking of my uncle's younger brother, who was very nice, and cute, I listened to my mom.

Most times I would pretend to like him just to be with my sissy, because I enjoyed being around them, but I knew that I couldn't marry him. Secretly, though, I was really quite fond of him. He was very nice, fun to be around, cute, and made it no secret that he sincerely cared for me.

Mama Gee always had the final say, and she agreed that it would be okay for me to go to live with Jax and his family, with the caveat that I would be with her on weekends. So even though I wasn't happy about the decision, I did what my grandmother told me to do. She explained that it would be best because he would help me with school and she wanted the best for me. And because I loved my grandmother more than I loved life itself, I trusted her with all of my heart. After all, she came for me immediately when I called in distress from hundreds of miles away. She was always there for me and always loved me unconditionally. This is something I knew because I felt it and because she told me all the time. And she protected me. Everyone in the family knew that I was Mama Gee's little girl.

Once I arrived at Jax's house, I immediately felt awkward. Like I wasn't really supposed to be there. He didn't even act the way he normally did, when the family was around. He just helped me bring in my bags and then sat down in his chair to watch television. His wife told me where to put my things but never made me feel as though she had prepared for my stay, nor did it appear as though she was even expecting me. I shared a room with the five-year old and the baby's room was right next-door.

My saving grace to make myself feel better was that my grandmother reiterated that I would be able to come "home", to her every weekend. And I did most of the time. Occasionally I would go to the college where three of the other brothers attended. According to Jax, that was to expose me to the college life. I would always stay in a dorm with one of their girlfriends. Actually, I think the reason for my going to the college was to keep Jax from having to drive the two hours to Mama Gee's and to also share my allowance money with the boys.

My dad must not have stayed away for very long because he started calling Jax's house to speak with me often. I didn't want to talk to him, but my mom told me how sorry he was and asked me to give him a chance to apologize. I did. He apologized profusely, and asked me what I wanted him to buy me. I told him that I wanted a brown leather midi/maxi coat, the one with the zippers at the bottom so I could wear either length. I received one in the mail by the end of the following week. He would also send me an allowance every two weeks. I noticed that every time I received the money from him, the other brothers would ask if I could come to visit them in college that weekend instead of me going home to Mama Gee's or to Sissy's.

It took a while for me to put two and two together. They knew that I had money, and they wanted, and probably needed it. But I didn't mind. I could get more if I wanted it so it was no big deal. I was happy to be at a college, and even happier to be away from that house where there was clearly some level of disconnect, that I later found out had nothing to do with me.

At one point while living in the house with Jax and Eva, I became very distraught and did something that could have ended up very badly.

One specific weekend I thought I was going home to grandma's, but plans had changed and no one told me. I couldn't go to the college to see the boys because they had other plans. Jax wasn't at home on this particular Saturday and Eva's sister was visiting for the weekend, as she did on occasion. Eva and her sister spent what seemed the entire time in the bedroom with the door closed, and both children in there with them, laughing and appearing to have a good time without me. I felt alone. Yet again I was all by myself. The story of my life. But what could I do? I had nowhere else to go and no one to call this time.

School had not yet started so I didn't even have any friends, only the girl across the street. She had a sister and a mom and dad and though it was never implied, I still felt that over there I would be in the way. I had nowhere to go. I decided that it was time to put myself and everyone else out of misery. I decided it was time to just put an end to my life.

I found a bottle of the over the counter pills my mom had sent with me in case I had menstrual cramps. I took one. Then another. And another. Until my ears started to ring and my head started to feel dizzy and the room began to spin. I laid down across the bed, on top of the covers, and I started to cry out loud. "Why am I here? Why doesn't anyone love me? I want to go to my Sissy's house. Why won't they let me do what I want to do? Why can't I just go live with my Mama Gee? I just want my Grammi. Maybe I should just stay here and end it all!"

All of these thoughts, and then some, ran through my mind. I had no one! All of a sudden, out of the blue, Eva knocks on the door to tell me that she had cooked dinner and there was a plate on the table for me. She might not have talked much to me, but she was good about making sure that I was taken care of and that I had every meal just like the rest of them.

There's usually one thing that will set a person off and it just so happened that it was Eva that sent me over the edge and into the feelings I was having at that time. The previous day, she had yelled at me for spanking the five-year old little girl, and told me that I could have paralyzed her by hitting her the way that I did. All I did was swat her little bottom with my hand. I was watching television while they were all locked up in the bedroom and she came out and pranced in front of the television and stuck her tongue out at me and then turned her butt to my face. I told her to stop it, she didn't listen so I swatted her bottom with my hand. I didn't hit her hard at all, she had on a pair of sweat pants, and she was a great performer, like me.

Everything got out of control as this little girl screamed bloody murder, which made Eva and her sister come running out of the bedroom yelling and threatening me with bodily harm for what I had done. To no surprise, I wasn't afraid of them, after all I had just fought my own father. They were clearly no match for me. I didn't react or try to explain what happened. I simply went to my room, closed the door, and didn't come out until much later. The time leading up to my near overdose.

While on the bed, before I closed my eyes to slumber, from out of nowhere, I heard a voice telling me to get up off of the bed and open up the window. I did. As if on cue, I started doing jumping jacks and toe touches and knee bends and running in place, before becoming more nauseous than ever before in my life. I immediately ran into the bathroom and began to throw up all of the pills I had swallowed.

Eva must've heard me, because she knocked on the bathroom door and asked if I was okay. I told her that I was fine and that I thought my menstrual cycle was starting. She didn't question me, just simply reminded me that I needed to eat the food that she had left on the table for me before it got cold. When I returned to my room, I saw that she had left pads on my bed. Like I said, she wasn't much for words with me, but she was very attentive to my needs, even when she didn't agree with my behavior.

After I got myself all cleaned up, though I didn't have much of an appetite, I went into the kitchen to eat my dinner. I saw my friend across the street, standing outside in the yard with her little toy poodle, so I walked over to say hello. It was also a chance for me to get some needed fresh air. My friend's mom asked me if something was the matter with me because my eyes were very red and glassy. I started to cry and told her what I had done. For some reason, I trusted her. She promised not to tell Jax or Eva, but made me promise not to ever do that again and to come to her house if I ever needed to talk. She was a nurse so she made sure I was okay before sending me back across the street.

I never told anyone else about that incident, and decided that I would stay alive, make the best of where I was for the rest of school year, and to go back to live with my parents for my last year of high school. I loved both of Jax and Eva's children, and though they are now grown and circumstances have changed the dynamics of our relationship, they will always have a special place in my heart. I just didn't feel comfortable enough in that house to want to stay any longer than I had to. I didn't understand then because I was still young, but there seemed to be a spirit lurking in that house that was different. And I didn't want any parts of it.

The family who lived next door to Jax and Eva consisted of a mother, Mrs. Lewis, and her son, John, who was one grade under me in high school, and a daughter, Wendy, who was away attending a private college up north. Mrs. Lewis talked so very fondly of her daughter's experience at the college where she was attending, what she was studying and even the sorority she had joined. When Wendy was home on her breaks from college, she would find a few minutes to speak to me, and I was amazed that she seemed so happy and focused and smart.

I'm not sure of the exact point in time, but it wasn't long after meeting her that I decided that I wanted to be just like Wendy, and go to the same college, study what she studied and join her sorority. And, later, I did just that! She never knew until over thirty years later, that she had actually influenced some of the decisions I made in life. All in all, I guess my stay with Jax and his family was one of the designs in the overall blueprint of my life since that's also the place where I met the love of my life, Eli!

116

CHAPTER THIRTEEN.... *My Guy, Eli*

We never know who is watching and how far they can see. Rebecca learned early in her life how people are sometimes used as vessels to help propel us through life. Trouble is, she never knew who this might be, never knew where they might show up, and never knew who sent them. Years later, she would finally understand.

Before I could think any further about college, I had to first make it through the eleventh grade there in that town, living in that house. Once school started, life became more bearable. As the new girl in a small town, word quickly spread that there was new meat at the high school. For the most part, the guys were gentlemen and didn't do much gawking at me. Some of the girls would look at me with a side eye because to them I was considered competition. I wasn't interested in being part of a click, that kind of thing never did interest me. Back home, I was in the same school for nine years with the same people so we really became one big family.

Soon after that first week at the high school, one day after the bell rang signaling that the current class had ended, I was walking down the hall to my next class when this boy said, "Hello", and asked if he could carry my books.

I assumed that meant that he wanted to walk me to class, though I wasn't quite sure, but I had seen something like that on television. Since he was tall, muscular, and kind of cute, I said "Sure".

I had actually noticed him before, talking to some other boys in the cafeteria, and glancing at me every now and then, but I never gave it much thought. I really thought that couples were already formed at the high school, and I didn't want any drama with anyone thinking I was trying to cause problems and mess up a relationship.

This guy's name was Eli and he was rather persistent and actually ended up being really nice and cool. He asked if it would be okay for him to come my house visit me sometime. Before I responded or even asked Jax and Eva if it would be okay for me to have male company, I first had to ask the opinion of my new friend who lived across the street. Just to make sure he was the type of guy that I hoped he was. She confirmed that he was indeed a "very nice young man" and that he wasn't one who had ever been in any kind of trouble.

With that kind of reassurance, I told Eli that it was okay for him to visit. I changed my mind about even asking Jax, since he was more like a brother to me and I really didn't see him as a person of authority. I was primarily asking out of respect since it was their home. So, to avoid pending issues, I visited with Eli outside under the carport. Though a few times he did find his way into the house. I was a teenager. And teenagers do what teenagers do.

I'm not real sure how we became an official couple but we ended up dating, and he asked me to his senior prom. My dad sent extra money for me to get my hair done and I told my mom the color of the dress I wanted, so she found one at a store there and mailed it to me. Eva had actually warmed up and had started to treat me more like family, as opposed to someone who was in the way. She helped me to get dressed for the evening and made sure my lipstick was on the right way. I didn't wear makeup and hadn't planned to, but she told me that as the final touch, that the lipstick would make me look even prettier, and she was right.

When Eli came to the door, he looked at me and said, "Wow"! I smiled, and probably blushed a bit.

That was my first real date. He had a corsage for me and asked if he could put it on. I said, yes, as Jax just stood and looked at us with no expression at all. I really didn't think that was necessary but I suppose he had something to prove. Trying his best to intimidate Eli, Jax asked him if he had plans to stay in that town. Eli had lived there for his entire life and Jax was actually the newcomer, so that was an interesting question.

Eli was quite the southern gentleman and went along with the game. He was from a large family just like Jax, having nine siblings, and was related to practically everyone in town. He never let on the fact that this tactic by Jax wasn't new to him at all. In fact, he was a little boy, and watched his brothers and older cousins do the same to his sisters and other girls in the family. He obliged and let Jax have his fun.

We had a very nice time at the prom and were back home at the time promised. Eli continued to come back to see me after that. Jax didn't succeed in running him away. As a matter of fact, Eli told me that he was going to marry me one day.

He was a high school senior and I was a junior, with one more year to go and I was definitely going back to my old high school. Once I graduated, I was going to be headed to the same college as Wendy from next door, and had no plans to move back to that little ole town. I was heading straight to the place up north where my life first began.

CHAPTER FOURTEEN.... *Returning Home*

While I was living in down south, I enrolled in the driver's education class at the high school, and was able to get my driver's license once I completed the course with a passing grade.   And though I left there in a hurry, I was anxious to get back to my parent's home.   For selfish reasons, of course. After all, I was still a teenager.   My dad had done a lot to prove to me that he was indeed sorry for hurting me and that he would never to it again.   As a teenager, I was happy to get all the gifts he sent and those he promised.   Especially the promise of my very own car!

After talking to Mama Gee about my feelings, I decided that it was time to forgive my dad and use the experience as a lesson for my life. I began to answer his calls more often and was pleasant while speaking to him for the most part. I still had a little bit of a stubborn streak and made sure that he understood that I promised to forgive him, but never said anything about forgetting. And I was young, so it was going to take some time for me to completely warm up. But since I was still a teenager, it was exciting for me to play along so I could get exactly what I wanted.

During one of the conversations we had, I told him that I was studying to get my driver's license, and I would need to

121

have my own car when I got back. He asked what kind of car I wanted. I said I didn't care, but it had to be red and white since those were the colors of Wendy's sorority that I planned to join also, once I go to college. He said okay.

Needless to say, as soon as I got back in town, not just the day, but the minute I arrived back to the house, my dad said, "Let's go", as he drove me to see what he had picked out for me.

He told me that if I liked the car, it was mine. Of course, I loved it. What teenager wouldn't. It was red with white stripes and had a radio. That's all that mattered to me. It was perfect. I drove it home and parked it in front of the house, since the driveway was where my dad parked his car.

When my mom got home from work, we hugged, but not very intimately, since we had seen one another less than a month prior. It was always like that with us. More of an obligation than real affection. Which is why I referring to her as *my mother* rather than simply *mom* or *mother* or *mama*. I really feel that since we never really bonded when I was an infant, our relationship was tarnished. I wouldn't understand until years later that it was all so much deeper than that.

My mother and I had seen each other last at the wedding of one of her brothers, who had married a young girl that was the daughter of one of Leah's guy friends. We were both bride's maids in the wedding which was held in the backyard of Jax and Eva's home. That was about three weeks prior. Upon seeing me this time, she hugged me, and then her brother and our cousin who drove me from down south back to my parent's. After all of the greetings were exchanged, my mother glanced over toward the street, pointed, and asked if that was the car that we rode in from Mama Gee's, and wanted to know whose it was since it looked so shiny and new.

All smiles, I quickly answered and rattled my keys with excitement saying, "Nope, it's mine"!

And from the expression on her face, she was not happy at all! She said she didn't know anything about me getting a car, and that she had only learned a few days ago that Beth's husband had signed for me to get my driver's license.

Here we go again, I thought to myself, as I looked at the expression on her face. Why can't she ever be happy for me? I'm not the reason for her not knowing about the car. They were the parents and I was the daughter, and their lack of communication was not my fault, nor was it my problem. For as long as I can remember, I begged her to leave him. Just walk out like I did.

"You don't have to stay here and subject yourself to this type of abuse," I would say. But no!

She decided to stay and blame it on me. She told me later that if she had left him like I wanted her to, that I wouldn't have had that car. It was always my fault. And it would be my fault up until the day that our relationship would no longer withstand the dysfunction. Until that time, my skin would continue to thicken while I continued to internalize it all.

The village was still at work, even after leaving for a year and returning home. With the Jacob's living right next door, I somehow felt connected to my grandmother, which provided the emotional security that I needed as a young girl. What made it even more special was the food they would prepare. I never knew what either of them did for a living. Back then, children were seen and not heard, and never had the nerve to ask a question like, "What kind of work does she (or any grown up for that matter) do?"

All I know is that Mrs. Jacob made the best greens I had ever had, and chicken salad that I always had to have whenever I returned home from college. And her husband cooked ribs that could be sold at any five-star restaurant. The other thing that made the house next door extra special was the fact that Mrs. Jacob's sister and her husband had ten children, seven girls and three boys.

Several of the girls, the ones closer to my age would stay overnight with their aunt and uncle for sometimes weeks at a time. They were so lucky. And me as an only child, I would get so excited when I saw their station wagon pull into the Jacob's driveway. I would watch as all of the children would file out, almost in formation. Excited. Finally, someone to play with me in my own backyard, and that was great for me, since I was only ever allowed to go down the street or around the corner. And that ship had sailed for me after that horrible experience. I never asked to go around there again. Interesting that my mother never asked why!

CHAPTER FIFTEEN.... *Life as A Kid*

Most times no one ever wanted to come to play with me at my house. My mother was rather strict about keeping her house neat, which made it awkward to move about like a child. Nor did she like to see people gathered in front of her house, even little children. She likened that to the appearance of a "bunch of hoodlums", so my little friends pretty much stayed away.

I didn't have the toys like most other kids. I had a few dolls, an easy bake oven, and a game or two but never really played because it got boring playing alone and I didn't have the type of parents who would play with me.

If my mom came home from work and found me sitting on the front porch with my friends, she would frown her face and look at us with disgust as she walked by us to get in the house. That would make them uncomfortable and most times, they would all leave as soon as we saw her my mom's car coming up the street. I couldn't go with them so I was left alone pulling branches off of the bushes and blowing the little white things off of the dandelion looking things in the grass, wishing for Mama Gee to come for me.

Later my mother would tell me that she didn't want to ever see that again when she drove up, because it looked awful.

She said that we looked like a bunch of hoodlums who were up to no good, and she didn't want us on her front porch ever again. But they couldn't come inside either, because that would've been even worse. She didn't like people in her house when she was home, and she said that I couldn't have anyone in her house when she wasn't at home. And I couldn't go anywhere. NEVER. But I just wanted company; someone to play with; someone to talk to since I didn't have my own sister or brother. Well, actually, I did have a brother.

My dad had a son who was born eleven months before me, almost to the day. I first met him when we moved from the city to the house in Belmont, but had only seen him once or twice. The story my mom shared was that his mother was very rude and disrespectful, so she was not allowed to call the house. But why couldn't Tyler pick up the phone and call himself? Why couldn't he come over to play with me? It would have been nice to have a big brother. Not that I needed protecting, but maybe the older boy around the corner wouldn't have touched me inappropriately if he knew I had a big brother!

Since Tyler had a brother and sister at his own house to play with, I just assumed that he had no reason to miss me. After all, what brother longs for another sister to boss him around? He didn't have a void in his life like I did. When I got older and was able to drive, I found where he lived. I would go to his house to visit him and his girlfriend. They had a baby girl. My little niece. I felt special. But I would only see them when I would go visit them. They never visited me or called me. It was always me hunting him down. Until that got old.

Tyler would ask me to ask our dad, who he called "Pop", for money for him to pay a bill or buy food for his family every once and a while. I would oblige. And Pop would give it to me, because he never said no to me for anything. However, he would tell me to let Tyler know that he could come over to ask for himself the next time. But he didn't start doing that until I was married, since I didn't come home very often after that. Only two or three times a year did I return home. Visits then were mostly for a holiday or to bring the children to visit with their grandparents, hoping they would forge the same bond that I shared with mine.

CHAPTER SIXTEEN.... *College Bound*

Rebecca's senior year of high school was really a blur. She only needed two classes to earn her diploma, so she found a job in an office working with a bookkeeper in the afternoons to help fill the rest of her day. Having a car really helped! And the extra money wasn't bad either. Most of her time during this year was spent preparing for college. This she did mostly on her own since her parents didn't really know what to do to help. Her mom sent money to her own brothers to help with their college expenses but that was about it for her. Rebecca's dad knew a lot, but wanted his daughter to know how to do things on her own so he offered little or no assistance. Rebecca felt, however, it was more because of her dad's disappointment with the choice of college she was going to attend, as evidenced by his not so nice comments.

Graduation from high school was over before I knew it. I was sad because none of the family from NC came to support me, not even my grandmother. It wasn't her fault, though, that her youngest son's wedding was the same weekend, which put her in an awkward position. I know she really wanted to be there with me because she told me and I believed her.

I was all packed and ready to leave for the trip to the college I would be attending. I had only applied to one college so I was happy that I was accepted. The trip in the car was interesting because my dad had registered our dog, Buttons, for an obedience class back in the city, because that was supposed to be one of the best places in the country for training a German Sheppard. During that time, it wasn't common for pets to ride in cars, especially for such a long trip. Personally, for a college bound, seventeen-year old like myself, this was not the way I envisioned the trip. Once we arrived in the city, we had to drop Buttons off first which was fine by me.

The trip was finally about me. We were off to the dorm I was assigned so that I could pick up my keys and drop of my luggage before heading to the main campus for the formal check in. Once we arrived onto the campus, my dad pulled up in front of the building where I was to receive my schedule and identification card, but didn't park the car.

I asked where he was going to park the car and he said, "I'm not. Go ahead, you are in college now. You'll figure out what to do from here".

And that was that. I got out, stood there and said, "Okay".

I don't remember hugs or any encouraging words from either parent. I do remember that I had asked my dad not to stress me about my grades once I got to college. Perhaps this was his way of letting go. Years later, I thought about the incident between that occurred between the two of us when I was fifteen, that point in my life when he was overly consumed with my grades, and figured he didn't want a repeat so he just let me have my way this time.

As I stood there waiting for them to pull off, my dad waved his hand and motioned toward the building telling me to go ahead. I turned and did accordingly. Once inside, I saw a lot of other students already inside and seated. The only thing different about them and me was that they had their parents with them and I didn't. That was probably the beginning of the end for me. From that point on I began to feel as though I was alone, yet again. So instead of trying to figure out what else I was supposed to do, I went inside, picked up my schedule and then called my aunt Leah. She sent someone to pick me up and I stayed at her house until the next day when she called one of her friends to give me a ride back to my dorm.

One good thing was that I did meet a friend on that first day who had chosen the same major as me. This helped tremendously because that meant we had some of the same classes, which gave me some bit of comfort. That first year was by far the hardest for me. I was no longer the smartest one in class, no longer the cutest, and no longer the one with the most anything!

What was likely one of the worse things for me was to be at a college in a city where I also had family. If I called, they answered and would come for me until I learned how to catch the bus. I started missing classes, and exams, and assignments, and everything else critical to my academic success. I never sent my grades home because I didn't have to. After that fiasco when I was in high school, neither of my parents ever questioned my grades again. Good thing, because they weren't that good. Not because I was performing badly, but because I wasn't performing at all.

By the second year, I had decided to try harder. Unfortunately, I received a call from home that the company my dad worked for was going on strike. He would be able to pay my tuition bill, but there would be nothing extra for books, food, or incidentals. I had to get a job. My mom was quick to let me know that she wouldn't be able to send me anything at all because she would have to pick up the slack at the house. I didn't bother asking if she could just send me what she had been sending to her brothers. Nope. I had to learn how to do things on my own.

I found a job at a local drugstore and pretty much worked full time from that point on. I missed classes and all of the fun things on campus, including the girl that my boyfriend had visiting him for the weekend. And my friends didn't tell me right away. Needless to say, we broke up. Alone again.

Tired of dorm hopping, one of my new roommates, Anna, and I found an apartment and our parents sent the money for us to secure it. One of the times that my mother was in town visiting her sister, she decided to buy furniture for us once she saw how bare the place looked. She couldn't afford to get living-room furniture and a bedroom set, so we all agreed that furniture in the front room was more of a priority. I had a twin size mattress and frame that my aunt had given me, and that sufficed just fine.

Moving so far off campus and away from others to help keep us connected academically was perhaps not the best thing to do. It didn't take long before both myself, and Anna, decided that college wasn't for us. To my chagrin, I called my mom one day when I was feeling like I couldn't take it anymore, feeling as though I wasn't smart enough to be in college.

As I sobbed between words, explaining my feelings of inadequacy, my mother quickly responded, and in a way that one would not ordinarily expect from a mother to a distraught daughter. "You know what, kid, you have had everything you have ever wanted your whole entire life. I never had the chance to go off to college and I have had to make one sacrifice after another for you to be where you are. Your daddy doesn't give me anything because it all has to go to you, so don't call here crying about how hard it is for you. Like I said, I'm the one making all of the sacrifices, so don't expect me to have sympathy for you."

Okay then. That was that.

Neither of us had a car so Anna and I caught a cab to campus one last time to officially withdraw from the university. It didn't take long for us to find a job. Making just above minimum wage, we realized that we wouldn't be able to maintain the quality of life we desired on our own.

After talking it over with her mom, Anna was the first to pack up and head back home. We found someone else to move in and take over her portion of the rent. Within the next few months, I followed suit, finding someone to take over my portion of the rent so that I could go back home as well.

CHAPTER SEVENTEEN.... *What's A Girl to Do?*

Rebecca quickly realized that the move back to her parent's home wasn't quite the answer, but what was? She and Liza continued to get along with one another the same way that oil mixes with water. Liza found fault with anything her daughter did. She didn't like her choice of friends, the fact that she would still be asleep when she left for work, and she didn't like the way Mason seemed to still give Rebecca whatever she wanted.

The way my mom would look at me sometimes was enough to make the average person run for cover. Yes, I was used to it, but it was really starting to get old. I knew that I should have done better with the opportunity that I was given, but I didn't. I knew that she wished she had the chance to go to college and would have done so much better than me, but she didn't. We could have gone back and forth all day long but those facts remain the same.

My dad was as generous as he had always been. And whether my mom understood it or not, I did feel guilty asking him for money all of the time.

There was this one guy that I met when I first got back to town and had dated for a short period of time. We spent a descent amount of time together so I had shared quite a bit of my past with him, including the telephone bill that I had left over from the apartment.

One day he called and asked me to come outside because he had something for me. I complained the most about having that phone bill which needed to be paid, so I assumed he was bringing me the money to take care of that. To my surprise, instead of money, he handed me a baggie that contained a handful of black pills and told me that if I could get rid of those, I would have what I needed to cover that debt. He also added, that if I needed more, to let him know. Not what I expected at all. Needless to say, I had a baffled look on my face as he drove away.

Later that evening I went to visit a friend and asked what I should do, and was told to give them back immediately.

"No, I don't want to do that, I don't want him to think I don't appreciate him trying to help so I'll just flush them down the toilet. He'll never know one way or another".

Again, I was told to give them back. I decided to do as advised. As I handed over the baggie in its original form, I lied and told him that my dad had given me the money, after all, so I was fine. Not long after that temptation, an older friend from the neighborhood, who had watched me grow up, gave me a piece of advice that more than likely saved me from a life that would have been totally different.

"You don't belong here. I'm not sure what happened when you were in college, but you need to go back and finish. This isn't the life for people like you. You have potential and you don't need to waste it trying to fit in around here." He continued as I listened attentively. "Now you know that I won't let anyone bother you, nor will I let them try to get you caught up in anything. But still, you should go back as soon as you can. Sooner than later."

With that piece of advice, I decided to call the guy who a few years prior had told me that he was going to marry me one day.

"Collect from Rebecca, will you accept?" is what Eli hears as he answers the phone.

"Sure, yes I will", he says immediately. Feeling no real need for small talk, I get straight to the point with the reason for my call.

"Hi Eli, it's me, Rebecca. I just wanted to know if you still want to marry me?".

Without hesitation Eli says, "Absolutely."

Right away I begin to share with him what had gone on at the house with my mom, and how things were just not working out for me since I moved back home from college. He tells me not to worry and asks if I needed money to travel to him, and of course my answer was yes. He agreed to send the money right away. And as a man of his word, when the mailman delivered the mail several days later there was an envelope with my name on it. It was then that I told my parents that I would be leaving. I just didn't tell them I would be moving to another state to live with Eli, a guy neither of them had ever met. Nor did I tell them about our discussion of marriage.

On the day that I had decided to leave, I got up early and began to load my things into my car. My mom had to leave early for work, and knew that I would be gone by the time she returned. Our goodbye before she left that morning was unemotional. She told me to drive safely and to be careful. I wasn't sure if she was sad that I was moving out, happy to see me go, relieved that she wouldn't have to worry about my every move, concerned about what I was going to do now, or what.

With my dad, though, I could sense a lot of sadness, as he sat in his recliner trying not to focus on what I was doing. He didn't offer to help as I loaded one thing after another into the car that he purchased for me when I got back home this time. After I put the last of my bags in the trunk of my car, I told him not to worry and that I would be back.

Although I told them that I was just going to stay with my Aunt Leah for just a short while, I think my dad knew that this time his little girl was leaving the nest for good. He pointed to the table where he had placed more than enough cash for me to use for my trip, extended his arms from where he remained seated in his recliner to give me a hug, and then reminded me to always call him if I needed anything. I promised that I would, and I definitely kept my word. I knew what it meant for my dad to be happy. He needed to feel needed. By me.

CHAPTER EIGHTEEN.... *Beginning of Forever*

Between what Eli had sent to Rebecca in the mail and the amount of money that her dad had given her for her trip, she had enough money to travel. And she went straight to her Grammi's house, bypassing the exit to where Eli lived.

While driving for what seemed like forever, alone with no one to talk to, I had time to think things through a little more clearly. Yes, I was anxious to be from under the reigns of my parents, my mom's judgment especially, but I decided that there was no way I could move in with a man. What on earth would my Grammi think? I had given Eli the number to my Grammi's house because that would always be one of three places anyone could find me. Either my parent's, my aunt's, or my Grammi's.

It was easy for him to locate me when I didn't arrive at his place as expected. He called each of the numbers I had given him before finally tracking me down. He had been waiting for me to arrive at his place for three days and started to worry when I hadn't even called. It took me a while to answer when he called because I felt bad. I carefully explained to Eli my hesitation to move in with him. To my surprise, he wasn't upset with me. He understood my feelings and appreciated my honesty. After talking for what seemed an eternity, we both agreed that I should visit a few times before moving in permanently.

Visits with Eli were always very pleasant as he was quite the gentlemen. He seemed to impress me more and more each day. He would drive up to the bank window and ask for enough money for meals and entertainment while I was in town. He would leave bright and early for work and then return home promptly at noon for lunch to make sure that I was okay and that I had eaten. He did more than his best to make me feel as much at home as possible. He was kind and he seemed to want to give me all that he could and then some.

My friends commented often about how lucky I was to have him, reminding me of that any time I thought of complaining about the least little thing. Not only did he have a fulltime government job with benefits, he also had two cars and his own apartment. Jackpot for me!

Although I hadn't completed my undergraduate studies, during the few months I was at my parent's, I had managed to earn a certificate in computer technology and had a pending job offer in another state. At the end of one of my weekend visits, I told Eli about my pending job offer but he asked me to think about not taking it and maybe looking for a job there instead. After thinking for less than a minute, I accepted his offer but told him that I couldn't move in with him without a ring on my finger.

I went back to Maryland to gather up my belongings from my aunt's house and by the time I arrived back at his place that next weekend, Eli was ready. He took my hand and led me into his bedroom and asked me to sit down on the bed. I did as he asked.

Reaching into his pocket, like a scene out of a movie, he then got down on one knee and spoke from the depths of his heart. "For years I have prayed every night, asking God to send you back to me. I love you and have always loved you from the first time I laid eyes on you in the hallway at the high school. I knew then that I wanted you to be my wife. I also knew that in order to have you, I had to make something of myself so I worked hard to get the job I have now. I never want to be without you again and want to spend the rest of my life with you. I want to be with you forever. Baby, will you marry me?"

Of course, I said, yes, and that was the beginning of our forever. We were married just a few months later because shortly after the proposal I found out that we were expecting.

Unfortunately, just two months after we were married, I miscarried. The devastation I felt is too much to articulate. But it took several tries before we were successful in our endeavors to start a family of our own.

I will admit that at one point I even offered Eli a divorce, as I felt inadequate to provide the family that a good man like him deserved. Because of choices that I made, I felt that God was punishing me and I didn't think it was fair for Eli to be punished as well.

Eli reminded me that he prayed every night for me to return to him and he was not giving up on me. He asked me to be patient like he had been and assured me that everything would be okay. But God!

CHAPTER NINETEEN.... *An Unfinished Task*

Going back to college and not stopping until she was all done is not what Rebecca had planned, but is the way it all worked out for her. Friends who had watched from the sidelines admired her perseverance; while family poked fun about her going on and on, joking that she would probably build a school one day just to have one to go to.

Eli promised to give me the life that I deserved so when he saw that I was feeling incomplete he told me that maybe I should go back to finish my undergraduate studies. We had moved to another state and were close to the college that I had attended. Unfortunately, with a new baby and the expenses we had with the new home we had purchased, we couldn't really afford it. Although Eli had agreed to leave his comfort zone and move with me to the big city, he was never comfortable there. With that in mind, along with the other situations, we decided to move back to the area where he had settled originally since the cost of living would be more affordable.

We put our house on the market, and it sold right away. My friends came over to help us pack and we were soon off with our baby girl Lela in tow, to our new beginning. Within a few months we had purchased another home and received our second blessing. On a visit to a doctor for a basic checkup, as the nurse handed me paperwork to complete, she congratulated me. I asked what for and she said that the test was positive and that I was going to have a baby.

I pointed to the six-month old baby girl who was in the stroller, and said, "Oh no, I already have one."

The nurse smiled at me as she pointed at Lela, "And she's going to have a baby brother or sister."

There were no cell phones back then so I had to wait until I got home to call Eli on his job to tell him the news.

We were both excited, but concerned at the same time. During my pregnancy with Lela, I ended up on bed rest for the last four months before she was born. She made it to term and was born healthy with no complications during delivery. With this pregnancy, the doctor understood that I had a baby at home that still needed her mommy, so he erred on the side of caution, requiring weekly injections in my hip for the duration of the pregnancy.

This worked well and our bouncing baby boy was born on the day he was due. I have to note that I went to the hospital one week prior to my due date pretending to be in labor. I wanted my baby to be born on my birthday, but was told that it didn't quite work that way and was sent right back home.

With our family now complete, I knew it was time for me to continue my journey so that I could be of use to Eli and not just another mouth to feed. Feeling the pressure of life and like

I didn't have much to offer, I packed a bag one morning and headed out of the door, telling Eli that he didn't need me. I told him that he would be better off without me and that I would take the small car so that he would be better able to transport the children in the four-door sedan.

Eli pleaded with me not to leave, saying he didn't understand my thinking nor why I felt the need to go. I wanted to make a quick exit while the babies were napping so they wouldn't remember their mommy walking out on them.

To my surprise, Eli woke both babies from their naps and stood holding them in his arms at the top of the steps saying, "Are you really going to walk out on us?".

When I heard my baby girl say, "Where are you going mommy?", I broke down and cried.

Eli came down the stairs and put the babies in their play pen and walked over to me. As he reached out to embrace me as I sobbed quietly, he said to me again, "Everything is going to be just fine. We will work this out, I promise."

By that next week, I was enrolled in the local community college for refresher courses and before I knew it, I had attended two other colleges and had completed my undergraduate and graduate studies. I continued until it was time for me to walk across another stage having earned the degree of Doctor of Philosophy. All of this didn't happen without a few obstacles here and there but my Eli was true to his word and supported me without hesitation. We even agreed to sell the home we had recently purchased to minimize our expenses so I wouldn't have to worry about working while in school full time.

Of course, this met judgement from a few members of our family and friends as well. But we didn't let that stop us. We were a team and worked very well together. Once, when I was about ready to give up because the pressure was starting to get to me, Eli got down on his knee and took my hand. "We can do this. Let me help you. Just tell me what you need me to do!" I couldn't resist the love and sincerity of his words so I agreed to keep pressing on, knowing that he would be with me no matter what.

Eli even let me convince him to join me on the academic trail. By the time we had finished, he had earned five degrees and was even in pursuit of a doctorate himself before he and I both agreed that enough was enough. He didn't actually need the extra education for his career, so I think he really just continued so I wouldn't be alone.

CHAPTER TWENTY .... *Family Reunions*

Family reunions were always fun and something she looked forward to when Rebecca was a little girl and even once she had a family of her own. Everyone would come home and all of the children would have such a good time playing with their cousins. There is one that she remembers the most, but for a totally different reason. That was when her mother made it clear that her brothers and sisters belonged to her and not Rebecca.

Liza was quick to let Rebecca know where her place was in the family. Though she grew up amongst the youngest of the Mama Gee's children, she would be reminded that she was really just a niece.

Early in their marriage, like most, Eli and Rebecca didn't have very much money. Family reunions were starting to be held in hotel rooms on the beach and not just at the house. Liza always reserved a suite and Mama Gee and Uncle Peter would stay with her. Rebecca, with a family that had grown in size to include an infant and a toddler, told Eli that they would stay in her mom's room also. Eli had let Rebecca know that they couldn't afford to stay in a hotel and perhaps they shouldn't attend that year.

Unfortunately, things didn't turn out as expected. Liza had flown from her home to her daughter's, to ride with them to the reunion festivities. Though it was never discussed, Rebecca was sure that her mom knew that they had not made reservations at the host hotel. After the ride to the beach to meet up with the rest of the family, everyone started to their respective rooms. Eli carried the bags for everyone as usual. He placed Liza's bags in the room she designated.

It was then that Liza looked at Rebecca and said, "Where are you all staying?".

Eli looked startled and just turned to head out of the door.

Rebecca turns to her mom and says, "I thought we were staying here. You know we don't have any money for a room."

"Oh. Well why on earth did you even come.?" Liza replies, with a smug look at her daughter who was holding the baby.

Rebecca turned and grabbed her baby girl who was standing by her side and walked out of the room to the hallway where her husband was waiting.

"Let's go", she says to her husband.

"Where?" a puzzled Eli says.

"Just come on." Rebecca says and walks a few doors down to her aunt's room.

After waiting for one of the children to open the door, Rebecca asks her aunt if her two children could stay in the room with her.

"Of course, they can. Where is your mother? Have you all checked in yet?" Leah asks.

To that Rebecca explained to her aunt what happened and that she and Eli would be fine, and they just needed a place for the children to stay inside. They kissed the babies and walked outside to their car and settled in for the night.

Shortly after midnight, and knowing her sister well, the aunt realized what had occurred and sent someone to look for Rebecca and Eli, finding them asleep in their car. They are told to get their bags and come up to the aunt's room, who had made room for everyone. She had rearranged everyone, putting all of the children in the room with her, providing a comfortable bed for Rebecca and her husband.

That next morning, when Liza sees her daughter at breakfast she says to her, "How dare you make me look like a bad mother! They all think that I made you sleep in your car. I never told you that you couldn't stay in my room. I simply asked where you were staying. Do you know how it makes me look to have you sleeping in your car? For once you could have been more considerate. Did you think for one minute about what they would say about me?"

"No, I didn't think about you. I was only trying to find a place for my children to sleep. Eli and I were fine until your sister came and asked us to come up to her room ".

In response, Liza simply looked at her daughter with that familiar look of contempt, which would make anyone else cringe. Rebecca did her usual as she held her tongue, turned her head and walked away.

Later that evening, as if things couldn't get any worse, Liza corners her daughter in the kitchen area of the hall that was rented for the reunion activities. Three of the brothers were also in the kitchen but were busy preparing food for the eagerly awaiting, family who had now gathered and mingled, catching up on what each did during the day. Many went to the beach, while others took smaller children to the kiddie amusement park, and the older family just sat in shaded areas talking about family members they remembered from years before.

"Everyone knows how awful you treat me!" Liza says to her daughter.

"What are you talking about? Everyone like who?" Rebecca responds looking as though her mother had totally lost her mind.

This was totally random and though she had noticed her mom peering at her at various times since breakfast, she didn't think much of it. It was just Liza being Liza.

151

"All of my brothers and sisters know. They all told me how bad they feel for me because of you. And you remember one thing. Those are MY brothers and sisters. NOT YOURS! And don't you forget it. And those are MY nieces and nephews. Why do you have them calling you "Aunt Becca"? That is going to stop immediately!"

"All of them said it? Really! That's interesting because they all seem to feel sorry for me!"

And then Rebecca turns to one of the brothers who was standing in the kitchen during the exchange between her and her mother, and says, "Hey, did you tell my mom that I treat her badly?"

"Uh. No. And I'm not getting in that. I didn't say anything.", the uncle says.

"I can't believe you just embarrassed me like that. How could you", screams Liza.

"You said they ALL said it so I went to a source. I can ask another if you'd like."

"They're not going to tell you what they told me. They are MY brothers and sisters and they care about me not you!"

Mama Gee appears from out of nowhere and says, "Okay enough is enough. Come on and let's get ready to eat".

Liza once again gives Rebecca that look, rolls her eyes, and turns and walked away. Rebecca shakes her head and goes on as though nothing ever happened though she is really confused and hurt. She was also embarrassed that her husband had to witness that apparent disdain that her mom seemed to have for her. But why? She had never known. And for some reason, it seems to be getting even worse.

Rebecca and Eli attended the annual family reunions even after that horrible year, but always had a room of their own. Eli made sure of that. He would never have his family in that type of predicament again. Liza continued each year with her looks and subtle comments to her daughter.

Unfortunately, as time passed, and once Mama Gee had gone on to glory, they did begin to feel a disconnect from the entire family. During the very last reunion they attended with the family, Liza's youngest brother insulted Eli by questioning the way he worshipped and telling him that he sat like a lump on a log and had no emotion.

Eli didn't take that too well, but simply responded by saying, "I don't have anything to prove to you, so you need to get out of my face with that crap."

The two of them have hardly spoken more than ten words to one another since. Family.

CHAPTER TWENTY-ONE... *Whose Life?*

I've often had times with my mom when I wondered, why? Just why would she do or say or look the way she did at me. Then one day she told me. As she stood on the screened in back porch of my house during one of her few visits, she looked out at the trees and then she spoke words that seemed appalling, but actually made me think.

From out of nowhere, she said to me, "You know that you are living the life that I should have had".

Without warning, Uncle Peter appeared unexpectedly and said, "For God's sake, Liza, what kind of thing is that to say to your daughter?

Without hesitation, she turned her head and looked at me with scorn and resentment.

With lips tightly pierced, she rolled her eyes at me, and responded, "What do you mean? I didn't say a thing."

To that he said, "Well I heard you say that Rebecca is living the life that you should have! That doesn't make much sense. You should be proud of your daughter."

At that moment, my mother rolled her eyes at me, yet again, and gave me a look that would have frightened most, and proceeded to walk upstairs.

We heard the door to her bedroom close and in there she stayed. This occurred late in the afternoon, so we left her alone until it was time for dinner. Uncle Peter asked me if I thought she knew it was time to eat. Therefore, as an attempt to appease him, I decided to go up to check. When she refused to answer the door, I quietly turned the knob and peeped in to at least make sure she was still breathing. She was. We decided to leave her be.

She did not resurface until that next morning shortly before the time that they were to leave to head back to up north to their respective homes.

When my mom came down to get her coffee, she simply said to me "Good morning", poured a cup of coffee and went back upstairs to get dressed.

Not long after, Uncle Peter came down for his favorite breakfast that I would always prepare for him when he visited. Grits just like his sister, my Grammi, used to make for him when he was a little boy. Though I rarely spent time as a little girl watching my grandmother prepare meals, I had somehow picked up the gift of preparing meals so deliciously that people would talk for days about how good they taste. Unfortunately, that was something else about me that didn't sit too well with my mom.

She never seemed to like when I was compared to her mother, but to me it was the ultimate compliment. She felt it was an insult to her. She often said to me, "I know you think I was a bad mother." While others find that an odd thing for a mother to say to someone she gave birth to, I find it quite normal. My normal. I had skin so thick that it sometimes made it hard for me to get along with people who I could tell were really bullies deep down inside. The signs were easy for me to pick up. Obviously.

As a young girl, I never had a direct altercation with a bully, and as an adult I find it hard to tolerate mean spirited people. When I sense it, I have been known to overreact. When people say that you never know what triggers the behavior of others, that is very true. For me, it was because I grew up in a household that was tense, with very little communication, yet a lot of performing. That is, when people were around, it appeared as though my mom and I were two peas in a pod.

Comments such as: "you're just like your mother" or "look at her looking just like her mother" or "Liza, she acts just like you" were normal for me to hear. That last comment, though, is what I have always worked so hard as an adult to reverse. After years of watching and listening and being the target of her frustrations, I knew that the last thing I ever wanted was to be anything like my mother.

I pretty much viewed the comment my mother made that compared her life to mine, the same way I had done any other comment that was the least bit unlike what a mother should say to someone she gave birth to. With a grain of salt. No reaction. I was used to holding it in and not letting her think that I cared. Though deep inside I really did. I would have never uttered those words to my daughter or son. My grandmother would never have said a thing like that to any of her children or to me. She was deceased by then.

My dad was still living, but it wasn't until several years later that my husband told him what she said. My dad's response was as it was on most occasions, "What's wrong with your mother? She is just an evil woman. She is never happy. All she cares about are her brothers and sisters. To her, they will never do no wrong". This would be repeated by my dad several times before he, rather unexpectedly, took his last breath on earth.

CHAPTER TWENTY-TWO.... *My First Best Friend*

Rebecca knew that her grandmother was sick. She knew that she would probably be leaving her sooner than later. No matter how much she tried to avoid the inevitable, she had to come to grips with the fact that her biggest fan, the one who she loved first, the one who always told her that everything was going to be alright, the one who protected her from the cruelties of the world just by being alive, would one day leave her. What would Rebecca do then. Who would be there when she called, to tell her a story simply just to make her smile, when life seemed so bleak.

When the call came informing me that Grammi had been taken to the hospital, I nearly fell to my feet. We were just there with her celebrating her 73rd birthday. She was singing and spinning around outside as though she didn't have a care in the world.

It had been less than two days before, that Eli and I were with her. Grammi called me into her room on that last night before we left, which was not an uncommon thing for her to do. We always had our special time together, with her sitting in her bedroom on her bed, having her time with the Lord. She never turned me away, though I would never interrupt if I saw that she was kneeling on the side of her bed. I knew that meant that she was having a serious talk with God, and I had respect and sense enough not to interrupt.

Grammi caught my attention this time, as I walked by her bedroom door. "Ria, come on in here and sit down. I have a few things that I want to give you. When I'm gone, I don't know what's going to happen to what I have, although I don't really have much. But at least I'll know that I have given you what I want you to have. My dear daughter, Leah, is likely going to do things her way, but while I have the time I would like to do this myself".

Grammi went to her closet to retrieve a small shoebox. Taking the lid off slowly, she began to explain to me that every lady should always have a handkerchief. She pulled from the box, three lace hankies and handed them to me rather gracefully. She then pulled out a lace address book that was given to her by someone as a special gift. It appeared as though it had been carefully handmade and designed especially for her.

"I want you to have this. I haven't written anything in it because I wanted to save it just for you".

I smiled, offered my most sincere thanks, and gave her a big hug as she handed that to me. Her dresser drawer was not far from the bed so she reached over to open one of the lower drawers, and pulled from there a t-shirt that that referenced the importance of working for the Lord.

Grammi used that time to tell me about her relationship with God and how good He has always been to her, and for me to remember that I can always call on Him in a time of need. She promised me that He would never let me down. This caused her to get slightly emotional, as she usually did when she talked about the Lord, but I held back my tears to keep her from losing control of this precious moment.

Before our special time was over, Grammi had given me almost all of her costume jewelry and her nice smelling perfume. I accepted the gifts in the spirit in which they were given to me, and told her that I would forever cherish everything that she had given me, though I still expected her to be around for a very long time.

Eli and I immediately got in the car to go to see about my Grammi. This was one time that he couldn't slow me down. I had to go to see about Grammi and let her know that she couldn't leave me. Not now. Not ever.

Grammi had been released from the hospital to go back to her home in hospice care. Hearing the word, hospice, didn't scare me at first because I knew that Grammi was a fighter and that the God she served would take care of her. I did know that Grammi was tired. She had an illness to take over her body about two years before this occurrence and at first, she declined any treatment by man. Her trust was in God, alone, and she didn't want a part of anything that was not of Him. The family was able to convince her to try one form of treatment. I remember going to take her to one of them and she told me then that she didn't like it and she wouldn't go back after that round was over. And she didn't.

Arriving at the house was hard because I was so used to Grammi meeting me at the door as soon as she saw our car pull up in the yard. This time I had to find her laying in a hospital bed in her bedroom. Not like she was just a few days ago when she sat on the side of her bed sharing with me the things and the wisdom she had for me. She knew then, I suppose, that our time together was at its end. I didn't want to believe it, but I had a feeling myself.

Walking into her room, seeing her lifeless was hard, but I had to be strong for her, like she had always been for me. I walked over to her bedside and just looked at her. The first thing I did was to touch her arm, and it was as soft and smooth as it always was. Her hair felt like the purest form of cotton one could ever imagine touching. Fluffy and silky all at the same time. Her eyes remained closed and her breathing was shallow. No machines, nothing hooked up to her, just Grammi laying there waiting for the Lord to open the gates of heaven to let her in.

I didn't cry because I didn't want her to think that I was sad. "Grammi, it's me, Ria. I'm here, Grammi. I love you and I'm gonna sit in here with you, okay. Okay, Grammi. You hear me, don't you? I know you do."

I took a deep breath, and I think Grammi did as well. There were no chairs in the room, so I took a seat on the floor, and leaned against the wall.

One by one, different ones would come in to say their goodbyes, but I refused to leave to give them privacy. I had to protect Grammi. She needed me to be there for her, like she had always been there for me.

Eli would come in to check on me often, but knew that it was best for him to just leave me be. He knew how much I loved my grandmother. I would keep forty dollars hidden away for the times Grammi would call me and say, "Hey, are you working much this week?"

That was code for me to get in my car, head south, and pick her up to come and stay with me for a while, which was usually every month or so. Working, or not, my answer would always be, "You all packed and ready?"

Grammi would say that it wouldn't take long for her to throw her rags in the little suitcase of hers, and that she would be ready when I pulled up in the yard. It usually took me less than a day to go pick up my Grammi. And with me and my little family, she would stay until one of the others started to miss their mama, and wanted her back. She used to say that she wished there was more of her to go around. She knew that we all loved her.

Anyway, as the day started to come to an end, so did each breath my Grammi had left to take. At one point I said to her, "Grammi, it's okay, I'm still in here with you. I told you I wouldn't leave you, remember?"

I know that I heard a slight grunt from her, though others say it was just her gasping. Not sure why, but when I heard her make that sound, I grunted the same way she did. Shortly after that, someone else entered the room and stood by her bed side, and Grammi opened her eyes. I jumped up, almost pushing the lady out of the way to let her see me. I wanted Grammi to see me if that was going to be her last sight. A tear formed and ran down the side of her face. I still refused to let her see me cry.

The lady that was in there ran out to inform others that Grammi was likely in that last moment of transition. By the time they made it into the room, Grammi was gone, and I had lost it. No more holding it in. Eli was right there to catch me, as he is always.

After the people from the funeral home loaded my Grammi into their car for her final ride away from her earthly home, my mom's siblings all gathered in Grammi's bedroom. I went in, only to find her slippers that I just had to have at that very moment. My feet were cold and Grammi always made me put something on my feet. She was gone so I had to do it myself, and I wanted her black slippers. I still have them to this day.

Aunt Leah decided that she wanted all of Mama Gee's children to hold hands and pray. My mom looked side eyed at me, and I knew that meant that it was time for me to leave. As I was walking out, Aunt Leah said that I should stay because I was one of Mama Gee's children also. I felt the tension in my mother start to rise, so I said no thank you and tried to leave.

"Becca, we need you here to represent the next generation. You are one of Mama's children and always will be. She loved you and everyone knows that. You have to stay. Let's form a circle and put Becca in the middle." We all did as Leah requested.

They all held hands, I stood in the middle, we closed our eyes, and one of the brothers began to pray. Within what seemed like a matter of seconds, I was startled with a blow to my head. Leah had hauled off and hit me in my head with her fist. I opened my eyes, as did others as they felt that something out of the ordinary had just happened.

Like it was no big deal, Leah does it again with her fists balled up and with a big swing, "You can't have my child. You can't have him." Another blow to my head.

Before I could hit her back, someone grabbed me. Eli heard the commotion and came running for me. He grabs me and removes me from the room with me crying and demanding that he let me go so that I could go back to get her. When I tell Eli what had just happened, he tells me to stay outside, goes back into the house and gathers our things, he put the children and me in the car, and we leave the house.

We go back to our home and return on the day of the funeral, and left to go back home that same night. I didn't speak to my Aunt Leah for three years. The family said that I was making too much of that ordeal and that it wasn't her fault, blaming it on the holy spirit. I told them that I wasn't sure of the spirit they were talking about, but the one I know causes no harm or danger.

My mother didn't understand why I wouldn't just get over it and let bygones be bygones. I never told my dad, because he definitely would have handled it and I didn't want him, or anyone else hurt or taken away to jail.

I did eventually forgive my Aunt Leah, but I will never forget!

CHAPTER TWENTY-THREE.... *No More Tears*

Rebecca's grandmother loved her unconditionally and provided the love that gave a child the security of knowing that if no one else would stand up for you, this person would. Forever! Until that one day in the middle of summer when the Lord called her dear grandmother home. It was on that day that Liza began to show Rebecca how she really felt about her, even though it took years for her to figure it all out.

"You pull yourself together, kid. She loved you more than she did anyone, and don't you ever forget it. The only argument I ever had with my mother was over of you"! What on earth was she talking about, I thought. I stood there as my mother peered at me through eyes that squinted in a way that might make anyone else nervous, speaking with a harsh, yet familiar, tone as she spewed words that have found a permanent home in my head.

All I could do was wonder why! Why was she upset with me this time? Why today? My best friend has gone home to glory, leaving me behind. She always protected me. She always loved me. She wanted me around. She said kind things to me. She told me that I was smart and special and was destined to do great things. Whatever I wanted to do, I could do. She believed in me when I didn't believe in myself. She was my source of comfort for as long as I had breath in my body. And now she was gone. I needed someone to hold me and tell me I would be okay and that my dear Grammi would live with me forever in my heart. And that she was not suffering anymore. That she was happy. That she would be okay without me because she was with her Lord and Savior.

"Why do you think that you always had to come back here each and every summer? And holidays? It's because when I told my mama that your daddy wanted to move back to his hometown in the Midwest and take you with us, she told me that the only way she would allow us to take you was if I agreed to bring you back as she requested. So, I had no choice. I couldn't tell your daddy that we couldn't take you so I had to agree with my mama's wishes."

Again, I'm thinking that this sure is a fine time for her to be opening up about that! I was so distraught over seeing my grandmother in that casket that I nearly pulled her out, so they said. All I remember is that as I neared the casket that the undertakers had placed by the door of the church, my heart dropped. In certain parts of the country, once the actual funeral service is over, it is common practice for morticians to roll the casket down the aisle and to the front door before anyone exits the sanctuary.

The undertakers then open the casket for one final viewing of the loved one before burial. For some, like me, this can be traumatic. I vaguely recall touching Mama Gee's arm and it felt like a cold piece of wood.

I must have screamed, "Who is this? This is not my Grammi. They put the wrong person in here. Can't you all see that? Where is my Grammi? Where is she? Can't you all see that this is not her?"

I don't really know what happened, or what I did at that point. I just heard voices saying, "She's going to pull her out, someone get her".

I screamed, "NO, I'M NOT. I just don't know who THIS person is and I want to see my Grammi!"

As I cried uncontrollably, my husband and others tried to console me. I remember my face being buried in the bosom of one of the elder ladies from my aunt's church who we all knew as "Sister". She was very well endowed and I felt myself smothering as Sister held me tight, trying to help me understand that everything was going to be okay.

My sobbing quieted slightly and I eventually said that I was okay and I just needed to find my mother.

Sister replied, "Baby, your mama is with the Lord now. You'll see her again one day."

As my sobbing slowed I said, "No. Liza. Liza is my mother".

Appearing surprised, Sister slowly loosened her arms from around me, turned me around, and pointed me in the direction of the big tree near the back of the church where my mother, Liza, stood.

I walked over, without a sound, but with tears streaming down my face, as my mother stood alone looking dazed, but without evidence of tears. She was always rather stoic, seemingly uncomfortable with the show of emotion, especially publicly. My dad, Mason, didn't travel with us to attend the service. I don't remember him ever even coming to Waters Edge with us.

Anyway, stopping just a few feet from where she was planted, I stood waiting for my mother to reach out to me with outstretched arms, like a normal mother would do seeing her child emotionally distraught, no matter the age. But not Liza! Her expression was anything but comforting, and her words were as cold as the arm of the person in the casket I had just touched. When I thought she was finished speaking, I just looked back at her, and never responded. I didn't say one word! After taking a deep breath, I just turned away from that tree where my mother stood, and headed toward the church steps looking for comfort from some loving soul.

I spotted Eli, who stood looking in my direction. He never had his eyes off of me for too long so I knew he had witnessed what I had just experienced. I walked over to him ever so slowly. He hugged me and for a moment we simply stood in complete silence. Our children, who were not more than five and six years old at the time, were probably a tad confused by their mommy's behavior.

Eli and I, hand in hand, walked over to them and smiled to let them know that everything was okay. They returned the smile and the four of us walked to over to where our car was parked as we waited for further instructions.

The last hurdle was the trip to the cemetery for the burial of Mama Gee. There, I did not shed a tear. I did not ask any more questions. I just closed my eyes and imagined my dear Grammi's smile and sweet voice telling me that she loved me and to be patient, because some day this would all make sense.

Without warning, the day we buried Mama Gee began a new chapter in my life. It was at that moment that I vowed that my mother would never see an emotional side of me again. I would never, again, put myself in a situation to have her disregard my feelings, and promised myself that I would never be that way with my children, or anyone else for that matter.

It was Eli, who later that evening said "Things are going to be different now that your grandmother is gone. We are going to see a different side of folks in the family. I feel it already".

Little did we know, Eli was right!

CHAPTER TWENTY-FOUR....*Grandfather's Smile*

As time went on, Rebecca realized that it's not her fault when the people in her life love and want the best for her. They offer unconditional love and support, wisdom, family history, and sometimes things that are more tangible, wanting nothing in return. Most parents are happy to have people like this in the lives of their children, but doesn't seem so much for Liza. And when it comes to her biological father, Liza seems to have a very big problem with the attention he gives to her daughter.

"Becca, Mr. DJ just pulled up to the end of the road" was usually how I would know that my grandfather was there to see me. I would get very excited and run to the end of the road where he would be standing with his arms outstretched. His smile and the gleam in his eyes let me know that he was as excited to see me as I was to see him. The visit wouldn't last very long, and he always managed to have a treat and a few coins for me, and a pack or two of cigarettes and a pack of chewing gum for Mama Gee. He maintained his respect for Butch and the boundaries that were set years before with visits to see his daughter, Liza.

Unlike my mother, I looked forward to the short visits at the end of the road and even more to the times when I would get to go to visit more formally with him and his wife at their house. I didn't have dreams of living there, like my mother did. I simply enjoyed hanging out with my other cousins who were closer to my age. My mother's older sister had four children and they were shipped to the country each summer, just as I was. We got along fairly well, with normal fuss that's to be expected with children our ages. Nothing ever required any of the adults to get involved.

The only time I had that good quality time with this set of cousins was at our grandfather's house, because Mama Gee wouldn't allow my cousin Gina back over to her house. Gina was a few years older than I was and I felt grown up with her around. That didn't sit too well with my grandmother, who didn't treat me like a baby, but she also didn't want me to grow up too fast. It was no secret that she was very protective of me. She watched my every move so she could see how much I seemed to enjoy hanging out with Gina. Aside from me, Mama Gee had all boys at her house now and she felt as though Gina was a little too advanced to be around the boys.

As I grew older, and moved into adulthood with a husband, children, and a stable home life, Grandfather began to dote on me even more. This eventually led to a kind of trust that some people actually took issue with. When Eli and I decided to have a home built, it was Grandfather who offered to give us the money we needed for a down payment. We accepted, but only with the understanding that we would pay him back. He agreed to our terms but would not take any interest from us at all. He kept such an excellent record of our repayment that we received a call from him telling us that we had paid our debt in full and that he would not accept another check from us. We were trying to pay some interest without him knowing, but he wouldn't have it.

As time went on, Grandfather started to liquidate his assets, or sell the land that he had acquired over time. He decided to split whatever he received equally between one of my cousins and me. I never knew the agreement he had with my cousin, but for me, the only requirement was for me to be available to go with him to his doctor's appointments, and to pay a bill or two if he ever needed it.

He had also made his own funeral arrangements and told me, "Everything has been taken care of so all you will need to do is be there."

Of course, I never wanted to have those conversations, as I could never imagine life without either of my grandparents. The unconditional love they each provided me was something I couldn't imagine living without.

Because he and my mom didn't have the best relationship, he never told her anything about the money he had given to me or my cousin, nor details of any other aspect of his life.

My husband, Eli, made every effort, but had a difficult time convincing my mother to just go visit her dad. She always had one excuse or another. Even when her dad had become so ill that he had to have someone to help care for him, my mother broke out in hives at the thought of going to be with him. When Eli would suggest that she go just for a day or two, she would look at me and in the usual bitter tone in which she addressed me, say, "You go. He loves you more than anyone else in the world anyway."

We did find out eventually that it wasn't just because of his love for me that she had issues with him. She was mad because he didn't let her live with him. She was angry because he didn't buy her the nice clothes like her sister, his other daughter, had. She was unforgiving because he did not send her away to college.

He was saddened to learn of all of this, when my mom decided to share these things with him when he was on his death bed. Feeling that he should have known how she felt on his own, my mom had never had a conversation about any of this before that day, but had held the resentment for him in her heart forever. Sadly, Grandfather told her that he never knew why she resisted him the way she did, and just accepted her for who she was without question of her attitude towards him. He loved her and did the best he could to show it.

Her resentment was heightened each time Grandfather made any gesture towards me, especially the older I got.

It was always met with a response of, "He's only doing these things for you to make up for what he didn't do for me."

Similar to the way my grandfather handled her, I never argued with my mom about her opinion of the way he was towards me, nor did I challenge her words. Deep down I always felt that his love was genuine and the origin never concerned me.

When Eli and I received the call that my dear grandfather had journeyed on, we immediately went to work to implement the plans he already had in motion. Seeing my grandfather laid to rest meant an end to the life I once knew. The road travelled to those southern parts would become a mere memory a lot sooner than I expected. I realized that with grandfather gone, there was really nothing left there for me and that part of my life was pretty much over.

The family was already beginning to act differently towards me for reasons that were never shared with me. One of my mother's brothers did tell me that though they would miss him, they expected things to be a lot better at their church with Deacon DJ no longer there. He was the last of the generation of those who had controlled the church for years. My grandfather's death actually represented a birth of a new era for the church that was originally founded by his father back in the late 1800's.

For me, I had only to deal with a mother who I had told everything. I told her about the land, the money, the bank account that I was left in charge of, and all of the information her father had shared with me. Interestingly, she told me that he had shared it all with her also, a fact that I found hard to believe.

The end all for me was about four years after my grandfather's passing when I received a call from my mother telling me that one of her sisters was having a hard time and needed some help. I told her that I was sorry but couldn't do anything this time. What my mother said to me in response made me scream for Eli because I was so appalled.

"What do you mean you can't help my sister? What did you do with my daddy's money?" she yells through the phone.

"I beg your pardon!" I said in response as I wonder where this is coming from.

In a tone that was the sharpest I had ever heard, she said again, "Where is my daddy's money?"

"You're driving it!" I exclaimed.

"What do you mean, I'm driving it. I thought YOU bought that car for me with your OWN money!" she yelled again.

"I used YOUR daddy's money and had to put the rest of MY OWN money with it to pay for it. I'm not sure how much you thought he left, but it was obviously not nearly as much as you thought." And with that I told her I had to go. I screamed for Eli and told him that I hated my mother and never wanted to talk to her again.

Rewind to a little more than a year after the death of Grandfather when I finally tired of the calls from one after the other for one thing or another. I had bought clothes for my mother and others in her family. I had purchased airline tickets, paid taxes, utility bills, and allowed the children of family members to stay at our house for summers and even longer if needed. After receiving a call from my mom about her car that she didn't like anymore and the innuendos about how well Eli and I were living, I decided to use what was left of my grandfather's money to buy her a car.

During that next Christmas break, Eli and I travelled to my parent's and ultimately purchased a brand-new car for my mother. We intended to stay as close to the budget as possible, but she insisted on having the one in the lobby so we said okay.

Soon after we returned home, we paid the car off, using most of the money we had saved of our own, and had the title mailed to her. I was thinking that by buying the car for her that she and the rest of her family would stop expecting help from me.

During that time of our life, Eli and I worked two and sometimes three jobs to maintain the lifestyle we wanted to provide for our children. We also had college for each of them yet to pay for. But like my best friend said, we worked smart so it never appeared as though life was as challenging for us as it really was.

Needless to say, when I received that call about her daddy's money, I lost it. That episode marked another beginning of the end of a relationship with my mother that may never be recovered. Not because I refuse to forgive, it's just that I will simply never forget!

CHAPTER TWENTY-FIVE.... *Mason's End*

One thing that was important to Rebecca was for her children to have the type of relationship with their grandparents that she had with hers. As soon as her daughter was born, her dad asked if she and Eli would let her come to spend the summer with them. Of course the thought was exciting to Rebecca, and she wanted her dad to be happy because he really did have a big heart.

As a little girl, I learned how to separate the feelings my dad had for me versus the feelings he had for my mom. Things I shouldn't have known as a child, I did, as I watched the tumultuous relationship my parents had with one another. Usually, I was just the liaison between the two of them, as they often communicated through me. "Go tell your daddy it's time to eat." "Tell you mother to pick up the phone." "Ask your daddy if he has any money for me to go to the store." And the go between would go on and on and on.

My dad might not have had money for his wife, but he always had money for whatever I wanted. And that only increased after my own children were born. From day one, he made it a point to make sure that his grandchildren had whatever they wanted and that they both knew that their grandfather would always get it for them. He told Eli and me to concentrate on school and work, and that he would do the rest.

180

He would tell us that he wanted us to have the best and that he would do whatever he could, and would work for as long as he had to, for that to happen. When he asked if the children could come to stay with them for a few weeks during the summer, the last thing I thought about was denying him that opportunity. Though he was in the street and hardly home when I was a child, he had since changed the course of his life. His family meant the world to him and he wanted to spend time with his grandchildren. More than just the two or three days we would stay when we visited during the holidays.

As the children grew up, Poppy, as they called him, would send them each a monthly allowance based on some formula he came up with. For birthdays and holidays, he would have them to send him a list of what they wanted and they were never disappointed. As they got older, I would stream line the list even though Poppy would tell me not to, and simply go behind my back and have the children to tell him what I had deleted.

My mom had issue with the money that was spent on them. She wouldn't block what my dad did for the children, because she had no control over what he did with his money. She would tell everyone all that he did for them, but her expressions towards us was an indicator of how she really felt. I knew that she had problems mainly because given all that he did for the children and for me, he never bought her anything. Not for birthdays, anniversaries, Christmas, or any other occasion.

I knew that she was embarrassed for anyone to know that and because I felt so bad for her, once I started to work and earn my own money, I would compensate by doing more than I should have for her. I recall once when I was a little girl, that occasionally one of the neighbors would inquire as to what my dad got my mom for Christmas. I would make up stuff on the spot saying that he had bought her a new frying pan, a lamp, or a new fur coat. They would look at each other sideways, knowing full well that I was not telling the truth. I didn't care if they asked her about it. Why did they care anyway? Nosey.

My mom never wanted for anything once I had the means to make up for what my dad wouldn't do for her. At least that what I was trying to do. Whether it was during a visit to see them or on her visits to see us, holidays or otherwise, I would always have a shopping bag or two full of whatever she wanted, or whatever I wanted her to have. She was always happy to receive the gifts from me, and it was nice to see her smile and not grimace or snarl.

My dad would call my house three to four times a day. But only when he was home alone.

If my mom ever walked in while he was on the phone with me, he would say, "Your mother is home now. I'll check you later. Bye."

If he knew that I was entertaining, which is something we did a lot, he would always want to know what was going on, how many people we were expecting, who they were, if they were cool people, what food I was going to serve and how I was going to prepare it. Once it was over, he would call again, wanting to know all of the details of how things went. Most of the time I would answer but sometimes I couldn't because I didn't have the time to answer all of his questions and get done all that I had to do in time for guests to arrive.

Rather than share details of all of the times he called and what we talked about, I'll fast forward to the day that I received a phone call from him asking me to help him find a dentist. He told me that he had an abscess that had formed on his gums and needed relief from the pain. He didn't want my mom to know so he didn't ask her for help even though she had a dentist that he could have called. He said she would be all in his business and then tell all of her brothers and sisters about it and he didn't want them all in his business either. I did what I always do when I can't help directly, I called my cousin who quickly stepped right up.

183

Unlike the way things had turned out before with no issues afterwards, this time was different. My cousin found a doctor, drove my dad to the appointment, where he was examined and given medication. Unfortunately, my dad was an alcoholic and that didn't work well with the round of medication he was prescribed, which ended up to his detriment. He didn't get better at all this time. Not even a little bit.

I remember hearing the phone ring as I was preparing Thanksgiving dinner for the usual twenty to thirty guests we were expecting. Knowing it had to be no one other than my dad, I asked Eli to please tell him that I would call him back. I just couldn't deal with the inquisition this time with so much else going on. I had way too much to do.

It wasn't until the next day that I talked to him and he didn't sound like his usual self. He told me that he called me because he was having difficulty with his bowels and wanted me to tell him what he should do. He went on to say that when he couldn't get me, he asked my mom and she told him what to do and he would see if that helped and let me know.

After not hearing from him for two days, I called the house over and over again and no one ever answered the phone. I finally called my mom on her cell phone and she said that he was there and that she had left to visit a friend because she was sick and tired of being mistreated. I told her that he wouldn't answer the phone and that I was concerned because he always answered for me, especially when he was home alone. She went on to tell me that he was sick and needed to clean himself up and wouldn't. Nor would he change into the clean clothes she offered him. She said that the abscess had burst and he was disgusting and the house smelled terribly.

I asked if she would call me when she got home and put him on the phone so that I could speak with him. Luckily, though, I got through to him before she returned. He had one last time to open up to me.

My dad, in a voice that was extremely hoarse and sounded like one I had never heard before, said to me, "Don't trust your mother. She doesn't love us and she never has. She only loves her brothers and her sisters. Remember what I'm telling you. To her they will never do no wrong. She will always take their side. I hear her talking to them and she lies on me and you. She tells them all about me and how sick I am but only for them to feel sorry for her. What about me? I'm the one who's sick. Just remember what I'm telling you now. I have to go."

I try to get him to stay on the phone so I can find out what's going on with him. I wanted to know what was wrong and what had happened over the past two or three days that I missed. Being so many miles away, I couldn't do a thing.

He refused to answer my questions and says, "She's coming in now. Bye".

Shortly after hanging up with my dad, the phone rings and it's my mother this time. "Rebecca, your dad is sick and is refusing to go to the hospital. I don't know what to do. You need to talk to him."

"Put him on the phone, please. Tell him I'm catching a plane and coming there tonight." I plead.

"Mason, Rebecca said she is coming to make you go to the hospital." My mother tells him.

"NOOOOOOO I don't want her here." My dad screams in that old hoarse sounding voice I heard earlier when he was speaking to me.

"What am I supposed to do. He can't stay in here like this. This is awful." My mother continues.

After all of the back and forth, I tell her that I will call her back and that I had to try to figure out what to do from here. Six hundred miles away. Eli, standing right by my side tries his best to help me try to make sense out of what was going on. I call one of my friends from college who is in the healthcare profession to ask what I should do.

She explains, "If he doesn't want to go, even if the paramedics come, they can't take him if he refuses. Is there someone else who can go over there with your mom?"

I realize then that I could call my brother, Tyler, to go over. After all, it was his dad too and he lived less than ten minutes away.

"Tyler, this is Rebecca. I need for you to go over to the house to check on Pop. My mother called and he doesn't sound too good and I don't know what else to do. Please, will you go over and then let me know what's going on?"

After about an hour, Tyler calls. "Uh, hey. Well he just told me to get the hell out of his house and to leave him the "f" alone".

Not knowing what else to do, I asked to speak to my mom. In as calm a manner as I could, I told my mother that once Tyler left, for her to go to her room, close the vents so that she couldn't smell the odor, close her bedroom door and lock it, say her prayers, and go to sleep. She asked what she should do about work that next morning. I told her that she is to get up at her regular time and go downstairs for her coffee like she usually does, and assess the situation with my dad at that time.

"If he is asleep and breathing, go on with your day. If he appears to be in distress or not breathing call 911, then call me and we will go from there." That was the best that I could do.

The following morning the phone rings and my mother is on the other end screaming, "He's gone. Your daddy is gone. He's dead."

"Okay. Who's there with you". I respond.

She tells me that the police and paramedics are there. I hang up, call her best friend, ask her to go over there with her, and then I call my husband to tell him. I also called my best friend. Within minutes, Eli had returned home from work and shortly after that my best friend was ringing the doorbell.

The next phone call was from the funeral home back home asking me what to do with my dad's body. I tell them that my mom and my brother live there and that I'm several states and hundreds of miles away.

"Yes, we are aware of that. I was given your number by your mother who told me to call and ask you. It sounds as though she is too distraught to make any decisions right now." The lady responds.

What about my feelings? My dad was gone.

The last of the ones who had come before me, who loved me unconditionally.

I remember my dad asking me if we would miss him when he was gone. I would tell him that he had many years ahead of him and that we didn't even need to talk about that. Maybe he knew then that his time was nearing, and was trying to prepare me. He would say things like, "You all don't need me anymore," or just offer encouraging words like, "I'm proud of you little girl. I know you're all grown up, but you're still my little girl." I didn't want to think about the inevitable, but life is life and my dad was really gone.

Now what?

My work had just begun.

CHAPTER TWENTY-SIX.... *Joy Overshadowed*

My family had just grown from four to five and now six. By all measures, this should be the happiest time in my life. Distress should be the last emotion taking up residence in my mind. I should be full of eustress. That good feeling one gets when everything is going so well that you have to sit down to take it all in. Not me. Not today.

On my drive into work, I called my mom as I did usually. This allowed me to keep our conversations brief without the possibility of anything coming up to cause conflict. To my surprise, she asked me if it would be okay if she came to spend the holidays with us this year. She said that she didn't want to be alone for the holidays this year and also wanted to be present when the baby was born, and thought she could also help them out once the baby arrived.

My daughter and her husband were expecting their first child to arrive sometime between Thanksgiving and Christmas. I told my mom that I thought that would be a great thing, but just wanted to be sure that she understood that she would be coming to be with us and not her family who lived nearby. I also made it very clear that we would not be travelling during this time, not even to drop her off down south. That's where most of her family resides and whenever she comes to visit, she begins to yearn to be in their company, ultimately causing a major riff between us.

No one could ever know of my apprehension. I only had a few friends with whom I confided regularly. I called two of them before I even shared the with Eli the conversation I had with my mother about her wanting to come to our house. To stay with us for a month.

One of my good friends was a not only a sounding board who would let me scream and use whatever language I wanted for as long as I needed to get it all out, she was more than that. She would scream and use the same language with me to make me feel better, even though she would say that she wasn't what she was doing. She would let me know that she wasn't agreeing with me just because she was my friend, but because right was right. Having listened to me vent for a few years, I knew she would let me know her true opinion. Given all that I shared with her, she believed that we should give it a try with my mom since she wanted to come for this special time in our lives.

My other confidant would always listen attentively, responding right on cue, and was by all means my biggest fan according to my husband. She wanted so badly for everything to be okay in my life, so she would try to be the voice of reason, offering the benefit of the doubt, unless things were so bizarre that her optimism couldn't surface. She valued mother-daughter relationships, and agreed that we should accept my mom's request as a positive gesture.

By the time I was ready to have the conversation with Eli, I had considered all of the pros and cons of the impending visit from my mom and was ready for anything he might throw at me. He did recall the details of our last visit with my mom. He reminded me that she was never happy being with just us and didn't want my feelings to be hurt if and when she started to show signs of wanting to leave to be with her siblings. I assured my husband that I had considered all of that and was prepared either way.

With Eli's reluctant support, I called to let my mom know that she was welcome. I informed her that with all that I had going on, she would need to make her own travel arrangements; another one of those things I had always done for her. I also told her that Lela was excited for her to come so that she could have someone with her since she was nervous about being a new mommy.

In preparation for the visit, Lela agreed to let her grandma use her second car, the one we bought for her when she was in college. Eli cleaned it up, filled up the tank, and had it looking like brand new so that my mom would be able to come and go and she pleased. We knew that she would want to see her brother and we had no plans of going to his house, especially given the way things were between us. Of course, I also asked my mom for a list of the items she would like to have while here and did my best to purchase everything she mentioned. My goal was for her to be as comfortable as possible, hoping that would help.

When she arrived, the first thing my mom did was to tell me that she really didn't want to stay in the bedroom that we had prepared for her. This was the bedroom that she always stayed in each during each stay with us for the past fifteen years. No worries. We made the transition to the room that she all of a sudden preferred. No questions asked.

Lela had made several trips to the hospital, and the day after my mom's arrival the time had finally come for us to camp out in the waiting room with the other families as we eagerly awaited the arrival of our new bundle of joy. One of my best friends rushed right over to be with me, with her pillow, blanket and snacks in tow. I didn't ask my mom to join us because though I was trying hard to keep an open mind, I didn't want her to bring the negative vibes that she usually carries with her.

My daughter had been turned away from the hospital one too many times and we needed nothing but positivity in the air this time. Eli and Andy hung around long enough to know that it would be a few more hours before the baby would be born. They both decided that we should all go home and come back in the morning refreshed. Of course, as mommy and soon to be grandma, I said goodnight to them both. My dear friend said she would stay to keep me company. She was right in her element, since neither she nor I, required very much sleep those days. I hadn't had much sleep of late, but that was okay. What I've learned as a parent is that you seem to get energy from the mommy bank in the sky when it comes down to being there for your children.

As the morning neared, our extended family began to arrive at the hospital. Word was out that Lela was to give birth any moment. All of the aunties and uncles that God gave them were in attendance, taking up their respective places, and letting it be known, one to the other, just how special it was to be there and to be a part of this special day for our family.

My husband arrived mid-morning with my mother in tow. She appeared to be okay but as usual was not genuinely happy for us. Like a teenager, she looked down at her cell phone and giggled and texted and giggled some more. I was never sure who she was communicating with, and I never took the time to ask. Those who have been the closest in our lives for the past twenty years wanted to go back to the room to at least wish Lela and her husband well as her labor neared completion.

My mom did get a chance to go as well but because there was a limit of two visitors at a time, she only stayed for a short while. Though my daughter and son in law never said, I can imagine the short stint was a tad bit awkward. Later that afternoon we were told that it wouldn't be long. Lela's best friends started to arrive and booted the aunties out of the room. All except one, and that was our good friend, May. She stayed while the friends were in there, at my request, just to keep "mommy eyes" on things for me. I needed a little bit of a break and wanted to at least acknowledge the waiting room full of extended family that had now gathered in full force. My mom started to question why May was able to stay back there and the limit was two visitors per room. I told her it was fine and went on to talk thank another friend for coming by the hospital.

Randomly, one of Lela's besties came out of the room and said that the nurse told them only two were allowed and that one had to leave. Of course, May stayed, so I went back to relieve her. We later concluded that my mom had found a nurse to tell that more than two were in her granddaughter's room, prompting the enforcement of the rules. It didn't take long after that for my son in law to call me to say that the time was nearing for the baby to come so I went back and relieved May.

"When I say push, I want one of you to hold one leg and one to hold the other. And when I say call the doctor, grandma, you pick up that red phone which will let the doctor know to come in". These instructions were quite clear as the nurse readied us for the delivery of our new baby boy. Once he arrived, I went out and announced the time and weight to all of the family who waited patiently in the lobby area. Screams of happiness erupted as we all hugged, celebrating the new life that had now entered our family unit. Once everyone settled down as best we could as we waited for the time to lay eyes on our new bundle, I noticed my mom on her phone. She looked over and told me that the alarm company was on the phone notifying her that the alarm was going off at her house.

She had been with us not quite one week and she had asked my cousin to go over to check on her house and water her plants while she was away, since she had planned to be with us for at least a month. All of a sudden, she stood up in the middle of the waiting area and started talking rather loudly to the person on the other end of the phone. We all looked at her indirectly, no one wanting to be the one to ask her to please take her call to another area of the room. Stepping up to the plate was our son, Andy. "Grandma, you can move over to the side of the room to finish your call since it appears you're going to be a while." That was not very well received. Who did he think he was, telling her what to do? He was a kid and he had no right to tell her what to do. Reluctantly, my mother complied with her grandson's request, but her nonverbal showed how unnerved she was with him. But, like me, Andy had thick skin.

I had been summoned by the nurse to go back to the room with my daughter and her new family to help pack up for the move out of the delivery area. Hurriedly, I went back to the lobby to let everyone know that the new mommy and baby would be coming through at any moment. Quickly, without cue, a receiving line formed.

Shortly thereafter, Lela, Drew, and their newborn baby were rolled through like floats in a parade while everyone applauded and offered congratulations and love to the new family. Once they were on the elevator headed to their new room for the next two days, I noticed that May was crying. She was always so very emotional so I went over and hugged her to thank her for the happy tears.

Before I could get a word out, my mom says, "She's not crying because of the baby, she's just a little upset because of something I said to her, but she'll be fine."

I went to May and asked what my mom said.

She sobbed quietly to avoid taking away the attention from Lela, and told me what happened. "As soon as the door opened for the nurses to bring the baby out, your mom told me that she was sorry to hear of the loss of my sister".

I was livid. Why would my mom deliberately put a damper on the mood that was so high? We were all so happy and she just had to spoil the moment. Her granddaughter has just given birth to a precious baby, which happens to be her first great-grandchild! Sadly, she couldn't stand to see all of our friends gathered here for the baby's birth and the genuine display of happiness. She was also, no doubt, uncomfortable since no one from her immediate family of brothers and sisters were present. We were never enough for her, not even at this moment in time that was the happiest for her own daughter and granddaughter. Her first great grandchild had just arrived. Why couldn't that be enough for her?

From that moment on, the air got more and more tense, thicker and thicker. As everyone gathered to leave, the new mommy let her own mommy, me, know that she was hungry and wanted pancakes.

After helping my daughter and her new husband to load luggage and gifts and our precious bundle of joy into their car parked in front of the hospital, I had no idea what was soon to come. All of the new baby stuff they had managed to collect after being in the hospital for two days following the birth of my first grandchild had to be stuffed in their car, along with their newborn baby. They were hungry, tired, anxious and eager to get home, and as usual, mommy was the one to help make everything all better. After all, that's what I lived my life for. Making things better for my children, like most other parents, no matter how old the children became.

We had prepared them for life but realized they did still need us so we were always ready and willing to step up when needed. And this is not always an easy task, because on most occasions, they didn't always know what they needed. But like most of the other helicopter mommies with grown up children, we seem to always know what to do and when to do it which is why I was right there at the hospital to help. All they wanted from me after we loaded the car with the baby, was food from somewhere, anywhere, as long as it wasn't hospital food. I didn't have time to prepare a meal for them myself, so off I go to make that happen some other way.

They were happy when I arrived with a hot meal for each of them from one of their favorite restaurants, and quickly reminded me of how tired they all were; and how they just wanted to spend their first day in the house together as a family. Just the three of them. I obliged and I left them in the comforts of their own home. But where was I to go? I didn't want to go home right away. My mother was there and I had a feeling something wasn't right. I have a sense for things that are not in balance. Perhaps because of the month in which I was born.

I decided to go to a drive thru and get myself some lunch. I didn't feel like getting out of the car and I was really in no mood to see or talk to anyone. After paying for my food, I drove through the parking lot and eventually found a place to park. I sat for about an hour, by myself. While trying to enjoy my moment of quiet time, I couldn't avoid all of the random thoughts that started to go through my head. I started to reflect on the relationships I had with the family I had known for most of my life. I began to realize what others had seen for years, but I would never acknowledge. I had been used. I had been had! The love I had for them was not mutual. For me, theirs was, and always had been, conditional.

CHAPTER TWENTY-SEVEN.... *Liza vs Rebecca*

Rebecca replayed that dreadful day over and over again in her mind. How did it come to be that she would finally get the chance to let go of the pain and hurt that she had felt for so many years? The betrayal. Deceit. Lies. Envy. Rejection. Pure jealousy, from the ones she had only tried to love, by sharing what she had been blessed with. It had all finally come to that boiling point for Rebecca!

My mother started to remember that awful day when she nearly lost the respect of her favorite uncle, the one who rescued her that awful day when her step father nearly took her life. As she stood on the screened in back porch that Eli designed for me as I labored to complete my post graduate studies, the envy within my mom started to emerge.

She began to let the words flow as she lightly snarled at me. I had simply walked out to the porch to see what my mother was doing. "You know that you are living the life that I should have. I should have the home, the job, the cars, the husband, the life you have. This should all be for me. This should all be mine!"

Little did we know Uncle Peter had appeared and was listening in utter disbelief as his dear niece spoke to me. His reaction caused my mom to retreat to her room without as much as a peep for the rest of that day and part of the next.

"For God's sake, Liza, what kind of thing is that to say to your daughter? You should be proud of her. You should be happy for her. Not saying things like that!" Little did Uncle Peter know that this added more fuel to the fire of contempt this mother had for her daughter. Just like the others, Uncle Peter adored me, and had even discussed the possibility of leaving his all of his earthly possessions to Eli and me. He also talked of having us to assume responsibility of his finances, and even mentioned to my mom that he was considering asking me if I wanted to be the co-owner on the title of his new car since he had no wife and no real relationship with his only child. After all I had been through with my mom, I let Uncle Peter know how much I loved and appreciated him, and kindly declined his offer. Once he passed away, I was able to watch from the sidelines. And I was happy to do so.

And then one day, five years after burying my dad, it happened. She had finally won. She saw that little girl feeling just like she must have felt for all of those years. The screams. The profanity. The accusations. Music to her ears as my mom stood watching my pain as I lashed out at the only one who had ever put her first. The one who would not let me take him away from her, like all the rest. Her real father DJ, her stepfather Butch, her husband Mason, her mother Mama Gee, and countless others all seemed to adore her little girl way too much for her to stomach.

Although he almost crossed over, this one person had proven his loyalty and was all hers. Though Mama Gee carried him for nine months, my mother always considered him to be hers. The pride she felt knowing that, though he had come real close to giving in to me, Liza's little boy, her first baby, her golden child, would never succumb to me like everyone else did; like all the other men in her life. My mother, Liza, would finally win. And I never even knew there was a competition.

CHAPTER TWENTY-EIGHT.... *The Sum of It All*

It was not uncommon for me, Rebecca, to receive a phone call from one of my mother's siblings. Now that I think about it, it was hardly ever just a call to simply say hello or to ask about my family. Always for something they wanted or needed and how I could help. I know other people do a great deal for their family, so this is usually no big deal. People will say that you should understand that when you give something to family, it's a gift and you shouldn't expect nor ask for anything in return, not even your money back that was supposedly borrowed. In most cases, though, it's a son or daughter, a brother or sister, or a parent. For me, it was really kind of different. I was married only months when I first started extending myself to family. Only thing is that these were not my children, my siblings or my nieces and nephews. In no certain order, the calls would go something like this:

"My son is a freshman in college and we are having a rough time right now. Can you help him to get his books, and maybe give him a few dollars extra? I know you are back in college now yourself and you have those two small children, but you all seem to be doing okay. I promise not to ask again, but whatever you can do will be much appreciated. And let us know if there is ever anything we can do for you all."

Me: "Okay. When do you need it?"

"My daughter just recently graduated and is unable to find a job. She's wants to go to graduate school. Can you help her to get into the graduate program at the school where you are work? And she will need a place to stay. If it's no problem, she won't mind staying with you all. Or, if she wants to move out on her own, will you help her to find a place?"

Me: "Absolutely!"

"My washing machine doesn't work. Your mother said she would help me to get one. If you get it for me, I'm sure she will reimburse you for it." "My grandchildren ought to have the same opportunities as all of the other children in the family. Their father is away for a while and I don't have the money or the strength to find a place for them to go for the summer. Will you put them in the program with your children and my brother's daughter and let them all stay with you. And, by the way, they don't have any summer clothes. And I don't have any money to send to help buy any or to feed them while they are with you for the month."

Me: "Not a problem at all. I'll take care of them."

"My son is graduating from high school next week and doesn't know what he wants to do with his life. Can he come to live with you and you help him figure it out? My wife of twenty years left me and she is sending our five-year old daughter to me for one month during the summer. Will you keep her at your house, and put her in the same summer program your kids will be attending? My daughter is in her first year of college and she is having some problems on campus. Her mother is not sympathetic so she called me. Though the college she attends is in the same state I currently live in, and you will have to drive hours to get there from the state where you reside with your own family, will you go to see about her right away, and call when you get there to let me know what's going on. And, by the way, happy anniversary! It is today, isn't it"?

Me: "Sure. ' No worries at all and thanks!"

"Me again, I was wondering if you could send me fifty dollars to help me to pay a bill. I promise to pay you back." Oh, and my daughter, the one who was in college, has decided to come home, but since her mother left me I only have one car. Would you be able to help us to get a car for her to drive? Would you mind helping me to get a job at the college where you work? And it would be mighty nice if you would help me to finish writing my dissertation. More specifically, chapters one, two and three may need to be revised. And that job I'm asking you to help me to get. Would you write the letter of interest, complete the application, and hand deliver the package along with anything else needed? Matter of fact, you can really just call me when they have set a date for my interview, and I'll come to your house so you can help me prepare. Good news, I got the job, and I'll be sure to let everyone know that my job is a higher one than yours. So technically, although it's not true, I'm your boss. Okay, now will you find me a house in the neighborhood where you live, and loan me the money for the down payment. Until that is ready, if you would write a check for the deposit on the place we will move to, temporarily, that would be awesome! And one more thing; I'm going to need to know what church you attend and the school your kids are attending as well. Since you introduced me to your college roommate, and we are now married because when I weighed her against the other lady I was dating, she won because she has a higher earning potential. And she is pretty so she will also help me advance my image.

"And just so you will know, when there comes a point that I ask you and your husband for help of any kind and you refuse, for whatever reason, I'm going to tell the family and turn them against you. You know how they feel about me. You know that I can never do anything wrong in their eyes, so don't even try offering your side of any story I decide to tell. If you do anything contrary to what I request, they will be so upset that they will come to town and you will never know because I'm not going to let you know and neither will they. As a matter of fact, I'm going to go as far as having your friends over to my house for a cookout, whenever I feel like it, and not invite you and your family. And, remember your friend from college, who became my second wife, I'm going to turn her against you too.

"You will never know why the tides turned...until she leaves me and tells everything. But that's okay. If you tell anyone in the family anything she tells you, they will never believe it. Not one word! Not only will I influence her, I will even go so far as to convince you to write a letter to my sister's husband asking for repayment of the money you loaned him. And when that hits the fan, I'm going to act like I'm hearing it for the first time. They will never know that I ignited the flame by telling your husband how they always want to have the fine cars and such, and to absolutely send the letter. This I will say after I suggest writing the letter and after I have read it to make sure it sounds okay. And your mother will agree and also suggest that you send the letter. And like me, she will act as though she is hearing about it for the first time when our sister calls each of us, distraught, upon receiving the letter in the mail. No one will ever know because you won't tell. And your whole entire reputation in the family will soon be shattered.

"And one more thing. If your son or daughter dares to apply to the college where you and I both work, I will do my best to block your son's acceptance in the master's program and I will ignore your daughter when she tries to introduce me to her friends during registration for graduate courses in the program which she is enrolled in at the same school. I won't help her at all! So even though you have done what you have for me and my brothers and sisters, your life will be totally ignored, and so will that of your children, if you even think about not giving me the fourteen thousand dollars I need for the down payment on the house in your neighborhood, a mere three blocks from where you live.

"Oh, and that church you go to, I'm going to join and become one of the leaders there. I'm going to make myself look so good that when they come to visit as a group during the family reunion that we host here in the town where you have lived with your family for so many years before I relocated here, no one will acknowledge you. While the church pastor is away, I'm going to have the guest pastor to acknowledge me, and our family members who are visiting. I'm not going to tell him about you at all. You will have to stand up on your own, after the fact, to let them know that you are a part of my family. You will look very silly at that time, especially when he says, "And what is your name sister?" Other members of the church, the real leaders sitting up front, will let them know your name when he asks. He won't know you because he's visiting from another state and only knows me because I made sure to introduce myself to him early that morning, before the start of service, so the family would continue to think highly of me and my religious calling.

"And when your children graduate from high school or college or have any other significant event, I'm going to do my best to discourage any of the family from attending. And they won't because I have it like that with them! You don't! Especially now that Mama Gee is no longer with us. One last thing! Anyway, my dear niece, like I said, I know you and your husband have done a great deal to help me over the years, and I didn't even mention everything, as its way too much. But you just try not to help me again and see what happens. I will even make your own mother turn on you. Don't believe me? Wait on it. You'll see!"

ME: In TOTAL DISBELIEF

I had never once asked any of them for anything. And, yes, I was disappointed that they were never there when my immediate family wanted or needed support. If not for the family that God gave us, my children would have wondered why my side of the family treated us like we had the plague all of a sudden. After all, for years, they had always been around.

As I replay all of this over and over in my head, what does any of it mean? Why has it bothered me for so long? Because I loved them and didn't know I was really being used. They were each part of my blueprint in their own way. It hurt. And still does. But I forgive them. And I wouldn't change a thing. All of that helped to make me who I am today. And if that's the path God had for me, who am I to complain.

ME: Lesson learned.

CHAPTER TWENTY-NINE.... *Final Epiphany*

Seemed as soon as we stopped giving, the word spread like a raging wild fire. The hurt and disappointment I felt was indescribable. As I think about it, the pain was more heartfelt because my own mother seemed not to understand why I felt the way that I did. She just wanted me to "get over it" and even accused me of wanting her to "choose" between me and her siblings. She kept saying that I needed to forgive. But I had. And I have. I would try to share scriptures with her that explained the depths of "forgiveness". But what she couldn't understand, or wouldn't acknowledge, was that "forgiveness" doesn't have as a condition or requirement "that you must go back to life as it was before". That you must go back to doing what you always did.

After all, my dad passed away unexpectedly and only one of them came to support us. And not one of the others called me. Well one did, my mom's sister, Leah. But only to tell me that she had known my dad longer than I did. She wanted me to understand that the hurt that she felt was, therefore, much deeper than mine. Didn't quite understand that one. Until years later.

My mother said that they called to offer condolences to her. But what about me, he was my dad. And what about her grandchildren who had lost the only grandfather they had ever known? My feelings were not just based on the fact that they had all seemingly turned on ME. It was because they then started to attack MY FAMILY. MY CHILDREN. And, oh no, now that's a real deal breaker!

You can do what you want to me. You can say what you want about me. But DO NOT CROSS THE LINE. MY CHILDREN ARE OFF LIMITS, and always will be. But they went there. And interestingly enough, not one of them seemed to understand why I had a problem, even after I took the time to explain how I felt.

As I continued to reflect, more things came to mind. My daughter graduated from high school and none of them came or sent a card. My son graduated the next year and they came (because they heard I was upset), but didn't talk much to any of us, pretty much stayed to themselves, and still didn't even give him a card. One of them made a promise to send something later, but later is yet to come. It was the same for their college graduation celebrations. No shows. My mom would ask if I sent an announcement of the graduations to them in the mail. No, I didn't. They never acknowledged them before so why bother.

I remember my dad calling me to ask me if we had ever received a card from any of them. I told the truth and said, no.

My dad then says to me, "Okay, that's all I needed to know. For years", he continued, "they have sent these announcements to you all and to us here, and we do right by their kids. But if they have never done right by our kids, from now on they might as well not send anything else here."

He added, "You know our kids don't need anything, because you know they will never want for anything. It's just that they like to know that people are proud of them, too!"

My mother thought that was so inconsiderate and told me that she couldn't believe that he would call me to say that. She only knew because she would eavesdrop when she heard him on the phone. And she could always tell when he was talking to me, because he seemed so happy.

The very last time my mom was in my house for a celebration of any kind, was just that—the last time! It didn't help that weeks before she arrived, my husband had called her to let her know how he felt about the way she had treated me over the years. She didn't try to understand his feelings and even turned bitter. Every bit of that showed towards my husband when she arrived, and for the few days she was in our home. Even our guests, our extended family, noticed that she seemed "a little different".

I decided at that point that I could not have her back in my home. I could not let her come here and make the environment so tense with her very presence. She would stay in her room for hours with the door closed and we would hear her laughing and talking on her cell phone. But as soon as she opened the door and walked downstairs where we were, she changed back into the cold and bitter person we knew her to be. My mind was made up and that was that.

But then, one week later I received a phone call in the early hours of the morning. Our son had been in a terrible car accident. Did this happen because I had said what I did about my mother? Was I being punished for dishonoring my mother? I didn't mean it in a bad way. I was just doing what I thought was best for my family, for my husband, who I love with all my heart. He is an awesome guy and will do anything for anyone, including my mother.

When we would visit her at her house, after driving for twelve hours straight, she thought nothing of having a "to-do" list for Eli. And he would march to the beat of her drum without one complaint. She even had Eli and Andy painting her bathroom one year on Christmas Day. We were leaving that next morning, and after all that he had done in addition to the painting the bathroom, she complained that they didn't paint the ceiling.

Eli reminds his mother in law that, "We have to drive tomorrow for twelve hours and I need to rest up. I will take care of it next time, when it's not a holiday and when we are here for more than just a few days."

She just rolled her eyes and said, "Humph!"

Hearing it all, my dad later told me that he didn't do anything for my mom, or give her much of anything because she was ungrateful. Unfortunately for us, we did all we did because of what he didn't do. Eli would build and fix it all; and I would shop and buy it all.

None of my mom's siblings came to see about our son after the accident, and neither did my mom. She had fallen in the snow in the backyard of her home trying to carry a twenty-foot ladder to the back of her detached garage. She was mad that the workers she had over to do some work on her gutters had left it where they did so she decided to go outside in blizzard like conditions to move it. She tripped and fell and the ladder ended up on top of her.

With over a foot of snow on the ground, she was lucky that she was able to crawl from under the ladder and make her way into the house. She was also able to drive herself to the hospital, where she discovered that she had broken her wrist during the fall. She had a cast on for a while, but it had been removed when we called to tell her of the accident. Yet she still used that as an excuse for not coming to see about her only grandson.

To be fair, I must mention that I did ask my mom not to mention anything to anyone in her family until I found out more details. That didn't mean that I didn't want them to know or to come. I was just protecting my family. Secretly, the real reason I wanted to wait to share the most intricate of details is because I feel strongly that some members of the family have a negative spirit and I didn't want any of that in the air as it concerned my son. I have my reasons for those feelings and choose to control the flow as much as humanly possible, as it pertains to my immediate family. I do this with anyone, not just with them.

My dad was deceased at the time of the accident. He had passed away three and a half years prior. I am positive, though, that if he had been alive, he would have been right by his grandson's bedside and would have made sure he had all that he needed to recover. We were fine though. Actually, we were a lot better than fine. As bad as it all seemed, it appeared as though angels were dispatched, one by one, to watch over our son and the rest of us.

One doctor showed up who was not even on staff at that hospital. When he walked into the room, he looked at Andy and immediately started telling us what he would do if he were the surgeon. He unwrapped the bandage on Andy's hand and looked at the finger that was barely attached. He asked the doctor who was in the room with him to get certain supplies because he was sure he could repair the finger right then.

He asked us to leave the room for thirty minutes and when we returned, he said that Andy's finger was just fine and it would eventually heal and look just like the other fingers on his hand. It was months later that Andy told me that when he was admitted, they had an order to amputate because they didn't believe it could be repaired. But God.

The same doctor told us that he would contact the surgical team to let them know what he had done. I asked if he could please help with Andy's surgery, but he said that he was just passing through town for the weekend and would be leaving early that next morning. I thanked him and told him we would always remember him for what he did to save our sons finger. The next surgery was to be two days later after the swelling went down on Andy's face, though this doctor said it could be done sooner. We were all exhausted so my son's best friend, Eli and I prepared ourselves to sleep in the chairs in Andy's hospital room. We were all exhausted but there was no thought of leaving Andy alone.

We were awakened at the crack of dawn by a nurse, who informed us that they were ready to take Andy down for surgery. After the team had prepped Andy, and had explained the specifics of what they were going to do, my son asked if we would pray with him. I said, "Absolutely"!

As soon as we said the first line of the Lord's Prayer, his best friend and his dad both walked away, too filled with emotion. I stayed and held my baby's hand. The nurse came to roll him down to the operating room, and I reassured him that he would be okay. He was nervous because he had never been in the hospital before. He had only observed the experiences of his sister. He had no first-hand knowledge of what to expect.

As we were saying our well wishes, I looked up and saw a man coming up the hall, carrying a backpack and a cup of coffee. It was that same doctor who appeared by his bedside. We knew then that everything was going to be all right!

Once they turned the corner and entered the double doors leading to the operating room, I fell to my knees right there in the hallway and cried out "Thank You Lord"!

Sooner than expected, the surgeons came to inform us that everything very well and actually better than expected. No complications and a speedy recovery was expected.

Back in his hospital room, Andy was a model patient and was very well attended to. As a matter of fact, one nurse even asked us if our son was someone famous, because of all of the attention he was receiving from the doctors. I told them that to us he is most definitely special, and that he is just a local guy who is loved by many.

I asked the nurse if she could tell us the name of the doctor who fixed my son's finger at his bedside, and had also assisted during his surgical procedure. She informed us that they had never seen him before that day, but he was the main one calling to make sure that they were taking proper care of Andy. She looked on a list to find his name but it wasn't there. Searching further, the nurse discovered that this doctor was, in fact, a renowned surgeon from up north, who had conducted major research and performed complicated reconstructive surgery on hands and faces. She had no idea why he was in the hospital that day. But I knew!

In addition to all of the positive things that were happening at the hospital, our friends who are now family, our neighbors, and our son's coworkers, showed up to support us from the time they received the news and continued their support until they knew Andy was out of the woods. Pastors from churches all over the city where we live were praying and asking the congregations in their church, radio listeners, and virtual viewers to do the same. I would run into people in grocery stores who would ask how our son was doing, and reassure us that they continue to pray for his healing.

Needless to say, all of this got us through his nearly five months of Andy's post-op recovery. His injuries required him to have reconstructive surgery, which included six plates put in to reshape his face. His mouth was wired completely shut for nearly two months, leaving him unable to eat solid foods or to speak clearly. He lost over fifty pounds and had to have therapy to help with his speech once the wires were removed.

Injuries to his hip required him to have plates and screws inserted, so he also had to learn to walk again, starting with a walker. He was able to leave the hospital after one week, and he was able to have the therapists come to the house for his appointments with them. Our family room was temporarily converted to a recovery room because he couldn't go up the stairs. This also made it a lot easier for each of us.

Through it all, we never had to ask anyone for anything. It was as though our every need was met in advance. Our friends who have become family, and our neighbors were with us at the hospital and at home when Andy was released. There was never a time when we needed something or someone, that I can say the need was not met.

Each person in the office at the company where Andy was employed, volunteered to prepare and deliver home cooked meals to our home twice a week. There was more than enough food to feed us, and whoever stopped by. They committed to doing this for a complete month even though Andy had only been on the job for just a few months when the accident occurred; and even though they knew he wouldn't be able to eat the food they prepared. They told us that we needed to keep our strength up to help Andy, and didn't want us to worry about what we were going to have for dinner. Aware of the minimum five-month recovery time anticipated, they also promised to hold his job, and office, until his return. He did return immediately after his recovery and is doing very well.

I realized that I was not being punished for dishonoring my mother after all. Accidents happen, and this time it happened to our family, and it all worked out and it wasn't my fault! It took my son to remind me of that. I even got over the disappointment of my mom not coming during that difficult time in our lives. I got over the disappointment of her flying over us, opting to join her siblings for their family reunion, even though she had not seen her own grandson. I still forgive her and I have moved on, but I had to realize that my husband and my children are not me, and they have their own feelings and their own way of dealing with things. I have had years of experience, so I'm at a totally different level of tolerance with my mother than they are.

Our daughter has had three surgeries on her spine. My dad was living so he and my mom traveled to be with us for the first one. The others were not as extensive, so as long as I called my dad and gave him step-by-step information, he was content not being by his granddaughter's side. With his health starting to fail, he wasn't really able to travel much anyway.

Lela's first surgery lasted nearly seven hours, as expected. Once back in her room, she lay stiff, and afraid to move. As my dad, Eli and I sat by quietly for our little girl to show some sign of being okay, my mom got up from her chair and said, "Well this is boring. Can we at least turn on the television?"

I said, "sure".

Just as soon as the first sound blared from through the speaker on her bedside, Lela asked us to please turn it off. She didn't want the lights on too brightly either. On that note, my mom said she couldn't take the silence any longer, and left the room.

By the time she returned to the room where her granddaughter was recovering, she was so excited to tell us all about the visit she had with a little boy down the hall. She said she had made a new friend. Neither of us really responded because we all thought it odd that she would leave the bedside of her only granddaughter, for any reason, and then have the audacity to come back overly excited about her visit with a stranger.

My dad didn't require much, and was a big help, juggling visits to the hospital and making sure his grandson was not ignored in the process. He was in the last year of middle school and the "big dance" was bon the evening after his sister's surgery. Poppy, as the kids called him, handled it all and Andy never showed signs of disappointment over Eli and I not being around to see him off to his first big dance.

I've also had a few surgeries over the past few years, and my mom never came to help out with me either. I was never bothered too much by it though; I simply rationalized her lack of support as the result of her having to work. And again, out of fairness, Eli is overly protective of me, making it difficult for anyone else to help much at all.

Overall, though, I seemed to spend a great deal of my life making excuses for why my mom did or didn't do one thing or another. It worked for me. That was until she decided to provoke me one time too many. No more excuses. The time had come for me to find myself a long- handled spoon.

And PRAY.

CHAPTER THIRTY.... *Letter or Poetic Prayer?*

The way I see it, my mother threw me away at five weeks old and never looked back...emotionally! To her I was a mere obligation. On her visit to my house, after not seeing one another for two years, I had hope that we might come to some level of resolve. I needed to know that she cared about my feelings. Does she love me at all?

The visit that I thought was an attempt by my mom to make amends, ended up being for her own selfish reasons. A time that should have been filled with joy and love and pleasant memories, ended up being a time in my life that I'll never forget for a whole different set of reasons.

After I arrived home from getting Lela, Drew and their precious baby boy settled in at their place, I get back to my house to find my mom hanging out in the kitchen, fully dressed and apparently ready to go somewhere.

"Hey." I say as I walk in the door.

"Hi. Where were you? I didn't know you had left out so early. I tried calling you." She says.

"Lela called early this morning and said they were being released from the hospital, so I had to go help them load things in the car, and then pick up some food for them."

"Oh, I see. I could have gone with you."

225

"Thanks, but it was easier for me to just do it."

Then it started. The big white elephant was leaving the room. My mom then asks, "Is there something wrong? You seem a little different."

"Yep. I'm exhausted. And actually, since you asked, I do need to ask you a question."

Right away I notice a tightening of her face as she says, "Okay, I'm listening. Go ahead with whatever it is. Hmph!"

"We can start right there." I said. "What was the Hmph about?"

"Here we go." She begins with that old school tone that I immediately recognize. "I should have known you were going to say that. You always have a problem with the way I talk. You really need to listen to yourself, you know. You're no different than me. Anyway, it was about nothing, okay. Hmph. Actually, I was just breathing and if that's a problem, then I'm sorry. Now what is it that you want to ask me. Just say it. Whatever it is."

"I really want to know why it is that you can't be satisfied with just us." I continue and promise myself that I will maintain a civil tone and not let her push me over the edge, though I could feel it coming. "This is one of the happiest times for our family and you seem to be preoccupied and don't seem to care at all. You said you wanted to come to be here to help

Lela. You went over there one time for a couple of hours while Drew was at work, and other than that you've been cooped up in that room talking on the phone like a teenager or something. Not what we expected. It seems like you just want to go hang out with your brother and not with us. As a matter of fact, where are you headed now. You seem dressed for something and you seemed unusually happy when I walked in a little while ago." And with that I paused to let her respond.

Without looking at me directly, my mom says, "Are you kidding me? I knew you were going to go there. I was going to have lunch with my brother and, if you have a problem with that, and I'm sure you do, then oh well."

"You can do whatever you want." I utter.

"I know I can. You don't have to tell me that. I am your mother. You have a problem with him and I know it." She says as she makes her way to take a seat at the kitchen table.

"Yes, I do. And you know why!" I take a seat across from her.

"Well he's your uncle and you need to get over it."

"I have told you time and time again that he is not my uncle. He is nothing to me. He crossed the line and has made no attempt to repair what he has done."

Beginning to taunt me, she says, "If you have a problem with him, call him."

227

"I'm not calling him. He has had more than enough times to reach out to me to fix things and he chooses to act nonchalant like it's nothing, steadily running my name down with you, the rest of the family, and who knows who else. I'm done and he is invisible. He doesn't exist. He is an evil man and I want no parts of that." I say as I look my mother in her eyes.

"Don't you say those things about my brother. Call him. You call him and tell him if you can't get over it." She continues edging me on but not looking at me at all.

"Fine. What's the number?" As I look at her directly.

Looking down at her phone, she lies, "I don't have it. I don't know his number."

Shaking my head, I tell her that "This is hilarious. You just got off the phone with him. You talk to him a zillion times a day. Really!"

Hesitating, my mom looks down at her phone and then starts to ramble off a number. I ask her to slow down and she looks at me and rolls her eyes, and repeats the number.

I dialed the number she gave me but he didn't answer.

The out of body experience for me begins at that point. "I told you that he's a coward and a punk and he's not going to answer."

"You stop calling my brother those names" she yells at the top of her lungs.

I then see her text someone and then my phone rings. I answer. He says hello and asks me what I want with him. Before I knew it, I had told him everything that was inside of me from the hurt that he caused me, my children, my husband, my roommate from college, his children, his ex-wife; how he had used me and how much I had done for him and his family and how I trusted him and did what I thought was right because he was family; but now he is invisible to me and will never exist in my life anymore.

Not really giving him a chance to respond much while I was nearly screaming every word, he did manage to get a word in at a certain point, just to say that he didn't know what I was talking about and if he had wronged me in any way he was sorry. Unfortunately, the sincerity of that apology was overshadowed when he started to go in on me, telling me how awful of a person I was and why I shouldn't be talking to him the way I was because he was my uncle. It was at that point that I yelled some not so nice words at him.

My mother was yelling at me from across the table where we sat, and he was yelling at me on the phone. At a certain point, she says to me, "I can't believe you would say such disgusting things to my brother. I can't stay here with you. You have no respect whatsoever." And with that she heads upstairs.

Having had enough of them both, I told him that he should get ready because his sister was probably leaving my house to come to his. And, also, I was ending the call, because this was a waste of my time and he would forever be invisible to me.

I called Eli to tell him what had happened and for him to come home right away since I didn't know if her brother was heading over to our house. Eli must've flown a plane to get home, because he made it in less time than it took for my mom to get her suitcase packed, and for me to gather my thoughts about what had just happened. As soon as Eli walked in, he saw my mom standing with her packed suitcase at the top of the stairs. He asked if she needed help. She said no. She then walks over to my pantry, opens it, and proceeds to ask if it would be okay for her to take the coffee, cereal and other food items that I had purchased for her.

Feeling almost drained, I ask, "So you're really leaving? You're actually leaving our house because your brother won't do what he needs to do to make this right with me."

"It's you with the problem, not him. So, yes, I'm leaving. You told me to leave. It's obvious that I'm not wanted here."

"Why do you always do this? What kind of hold does he have on you. Why do you always make sides, and then take his? This doesn't make any sense to me at all. My first grand baby was born yesterday. You asked to come here to be with us. This is a happy time in our lives. You ought to be celebrating with us. Instead you pick a fight with me and then pack your bags to leave. Are you sure this is what you want to really want to do?"

"Yes," is all my mother says to me in response to all of that. "Yes."

"Well don't you lie and tell anyone that we forced you to go, because this is your decision. You are choosing to do this on your own. LORD HAVE MERCY!" was just about all I had left to say to her.

She looks away from me and says nothing in response.

Not sure of what was going to happen next, I ask, "Do you have a ride coming for you?"

I had to ask because we had Lela's car here for her to use, and didn't know if she had made plans to drive that or if her brother was coming to pick her up.

She looks at Eli, still avoiding eye contact with me, and says, "Will you take me? Please?"

Eli nods, yes, and picks up her suitcase without asking if she needed him to do so. He looks at me and tells me that he would be right back. Uncomfortable with him going alone, even though it was just around the corner, I told him that I would ride with them.

231

While in the van, I turned to look at my mom and again asked her if she was sure she wanted to leave. Staring out of the window, she says yes. I told her that it was my hope that one day she would see her brother for the evil man he was. He had turned the whole family against me, including her, all because we wouldn't give him an exorbitant amount of money to help with a down payment on his house. I told her that I would continue to pray for her, specifically for her to recognize her brother for who he was before it was too late.

We pulled up in the driveway. Eli got out first to get my mom's belongings. Right away, her brother comes out of the front door and stands on the porch with his cell phone in hand. Noticing that my mom was struggling to open the door of the van, I get out to help her. When she gets out completely, she asks me for a hug. I oblige. She extends her arms to hug Eli, but he turns away. Watching my mom walk toward the steps where her brother stood with an evil smirk on his face, sent me to a place that I hope to never go again.

I began to yell and scream at him, telling him how evil he was and how I hoped he was finally happy. I told him that I was going to pray for him because he was a lost soul. My word choice was of the secular world, and that's all I'll say about that. I don't really remember much other than my husband grabbing me as I lunged towards the porch where my mother stood with her brother, both with their arms around the another.

All I remember is her brother's look and her words, "OH MY GOD! How could you talk to my brother like this? You are an awful person! I can't believe you. WHO ARE YOU?" Words from a mother as she watched her only child painfully release all that she had inside to one who had hurt her so terribly bad. As Eli forced me into the car, we both watched as the two of them walked in the house, closed the door, and locked it.

Later that day, my mother called and asked me for some medication for fluid retention that was prescribed for me. I told her that I didn't know where it was. She said that she couldn't find hers either and that her ankles were swelling. I suggested that she call her doctor for a refill. She said, okay, and hung up. She remained with her brother for the next three weeks.

They did go down south for the holiday and returned back to his house, where she stayed until she was able to get a flight to take her back to Belmont. During the time when she was only three blocks away from my door, my mom didn't call me again, she didn't knock on my door, nor did she see either of her grandchildren.

The morning after all of this occurred, I decided to compose a letter to my mother telling her how I felt about everything. This ended up being another out of body experience, because by the time I had finished I had no idea what I had written. It was too long for a text, so I saved it to my notes.

What is it about me? Why does my mother not want to be with the only one who would love and care for her, if given the opportunity? Why does she push me away, emotionally, time and time again? Is it okay for me not to care anymore? How many chances must I allow for my feelings to be trampled on? What do I really expect from her? There has to be something more? Grammi said to pray and that God would answer. He would give me the desires of my heart. After putting it all together in the letter that was never mailed, I hoped that answers would come sooner than later.

"SPECIAL LETTER TO MY MOTHER"

You got pregnant with me and you began your walk of shame.
You gave birth to me, your loss of freedom, I was to blame.
You cried when I cried, because you never wanted this.
All you could stand to think about, was the life you would miss.

Your mother said to you, just bring your baby to me, my child; and to
that you did oblige, without the least bit of heartfelt pain.
All you could imagine or think about was with me gone, you could
finally live again.

On the bus, you carried me, a mere five-week old baby swaddled.
When the driver announced the town you had recently fled, you
grabbed my blanket and bottle.

Without stepping foot off of the bus, you handed me off to the step-
father you did always dread.
He took me from you, with bottle and blanket, then quickly covered my
head.

From that day forward, you promised yourself that a burden I would
never be; you found a man at some point, and you gave me his name.
There was never real love there, between you two, just a shelter for
your lustful shame.

Another baby was to form to quickly seal that deal for you.
Sadly, he didn't quite make it, for what reason you had no clue.

There was no heartfelt hurt when the doctors said, "children you
should no longer bear."
Words to your ears, you'll never admit, because you didn't really care.

Soon after meeting that handsome beau, you two eventually wed.
A relationship from hell, another man to dread.

Four years later, he said to you, "go get my little girl.
I want her with me, for she is my world."
Your mind started again regret.
That lustful day that seed of life was set.

Whose child is she really, was the silent question asked by many.
Sleeping dogs were made to lie, so answers, there weren't any.

Only you and God could dare reveal; all others are now with Thee.
One day when we're all there, we may finally know; answers mostly
just for me!

More than half century later, you still have that shame.
That precious baby girl is still to blame.
How could her life be so perfect, through eyes of those so bitter?
Let's all band together so see if she will wither.
I'll blame her for everything until the day I die.
And believe in my heart, she will never know why.

Yet she does know why, but God's grace and mercy have kept her from
that pain.
You see, your mother talked to God long ago and asked Him to refrain.
From letting her be hurt from any harm or danger or bitter feelings
from others
Not just from you, but also from your sisters and your brothers.

Yes, half a century later, this little girl has grown to be.
A person you will never know because you never wanted to see.
Her for who she really was, God's precious gift sent from above.
For others, not just you, someone special to love.

So, thank you my dear mother for finally helping me understand, on
that one dreadful day.
It's not me who chose, it's you, in your own peculiar way!

That day I did scream, I did shout words so cruel, harsh and bitter to "that thing" as I now call him.
As I emptied all hurt once held inside, in a way, to you, so grim.

For a brief day or two thereafter, God rested my voice slightly for me.
Had the chance to look in the mirror, so I really now can see!

I know now I have no loss; you see, God gave me a family, a circle so big and so sweet.
A village of people who love me for me, no condition, nothing material or monetary, am I required to meet.

Those with whom I feel love and who help keep me protected.
From dangers seen and unseen, especially those least expected.

That man who gave me his name told me time and time again, even before taking his final breath, "your mother will never love you the way she does her sisters and her brothers."
What you may not realize is that it's really just biology, because I always knew you never gave me your heart, not truly as a mother.

He told me that to you, "that thing" "would never do no wrong; he's her first little baby, her little golden child.
Fret not, dear daughter, when on that day you see, your name to them and to others defiled."

Also, my dear daughter when the final rejection comes from the one you know as your mother.
Remember that God gave you me, to love and protect you, and not just me, there are countless others.

How fitting it would be that this would occur exactly five years from the day the man I knew as my dad on earth and in my heart.

237

*Would leave this old world, leaving me still to wonder whose seed was
really planted giving me my life's start!*

*A lesson so hard, so bitter, yet sweet, will help mold you to be.
The kind and loving friend, wife, and mother to those who remind you
of me.
Words I hear now from my dear grandmother's spirit, as I cross over
to a new stage of life.
I will love and cherish my new grand-baby too, the way your mother
did me-for you, without any strife!*

*I'm not mad, angry or sad, just a tad disappointed, you see.
I tried and I tried to find the mother in you, who might be there for me.
To be honest, we both know it was never really there, so we really can't
miss what we never had.
So, enjoy your time with ones for whom you truly care, and please
don't be ill or sad.*

*It's finally over now, dear mother, no more hurt, shame or blame.
I'm not sorry you were here; actually, glad you came.
For this trip did reveal what as an infant I knew.
One can never love the product of lust, that awful day for you!*

*"How could you?" you're thinking as you read each and every line.
But that little boy that day was a necessary sign.
He needed to come to ignite that flame.
To finally shed light on that lustful shame.*

*"I CAN'T BELIEVE THIS," you're saying to yourself, not doubt!
It's okay, my dear mother, I finally got it all out.
So now, from me to you, the torch has been passed.
You may continue to bury this memory, or admit the truth at last!*

Sincerely, Rebecca

*After writing this letter I realized that it was never intended for my mother, but was instead a prayer to God, because it was He who answered me. Not sure if I was quite ready for the answer, but I needed to know, and Grammi always said that God would give me the desires of my heart. She said that all I had to do was ask. Funny thing is that during the time while I was composing that letter, my heart was in its own zone and I didn't realize what I had written until I read it out loud to Eli.

As soon as Eli arrived home from work the day I had composed all of my thoughts to my mother, without giving him a chance to sit down, I said, "I need you to read something. Better yet, let me read it to you so that I can hear it as well."

Once I finished reading, "Wow!" is all he said.

As I did when I felt the need for guidance, I went straight to Annie and her husband Felix, who Eli and I have grown to love and appreciate for the wisdom they offer selflessly and without bias. They have counseled us many times, especially when we get a little confused with one another.

"Okay, I need help. I need for the both of you to read something for me and tell me what to do."

After reading, they both looked up at me, both agreeing that the letter was poetic and very well written, but should not be mailed to my mother. Felix asked what I hoped to gain by mailing it, and they both felt as though the letter would not be received in the same spirit in which it was written. I did as they suggested and put the letter away in my special hiding place. My heart.

My mother never had the chance to respond to my question, but God did. One month later as Eli and I were at lunch with Andy, Lela and our new bundle of joy, in celebration of him turning one month old, my phone rang from an unknown number. It bore the same area code as the one in the city where my mother lived. I made the decision to let it go to voice mail and listened as soon as the message was left.

"Hello, this message is for Rebecca. This is Sara calling from the county treasurer's office in Belmont. If you could call me back as soon as possible, I have a question regarding some property you may be an heir to."

"What in the world?" I said out loud and immediately hit the call back button on my cell phone.

"Hi Sara, this is Rebecca returning your call."

"Yes, Rebecca. I just needed to clear up a few things before we proceed with a claim that has been made on a piece of property. I understand that Mason Parks was your dad, is that correct?"

"Yes." I replied.

"Okay, well I just needed to verify that with you because we spoke previously to a Liza Parks, who I believe is your mother."

"Yes, Liza Parks is my mother."

"We needed to hear from you because according to the records we were able to pull up, from Mason's obituary, he had two children. But when we spoke with Liza, she informed us that Mason had only one biological child and his name was Tyler."

I nearly dropped the phone and said to my family that they needed to hear what I had just heard.

Putting the phone on speaker, and not caring who else in the restaurant might also hear, I said, "Sara, would you mind repeating that one more time. I couldn't quite hear you."

"No problem. I just needed to verify that Mason was indeed your dad because we have on record from Liza Parks that he was not."

Eyes widened, forks dropped, gasps were made as my family also heard the most shocking news ever. Mason was NOT my biological father. He only had one child and it wasn't me.

"Sara, I'm at a luncheon and will need to call you back. Will you be available in the next fifteen to thirty minutes?"

"Absolutely, I will wait to hear from you." And with that, the call ended and the lives of each of us sitting at that table was forever changed.

After regaining my composure, I walk out to my car to call Sara once again. "Hi, this is Rebecca, again. I apologize for not being able to talk earlier, but would you mind telling me again what my mother told you?"

"Oh, I'm so sorry, did I share something I shouldn't have? I just assumed..."

Cutting her off mid-sentence, "Not at all, Sara. My mother and I are somewhat estranged, so she's liable to say just about anything these days."

"Alright. I want to let you know as well that we do have a recording of the conversation with your mother. We keep the recordings on file for obvious reasons. As a matter, we spoke with her about three months ago, and it was actually on your birthday."

"Really, how do you know the date of my birthday?"

"There is a quite extensive database online that we use, which has demographics recorded. That's why we needed to speak with you, because of the inconsistencies. You were listed in the obituary for Mason Parks, but you're not listed anywhere else. The only listing we have for a child under the name of Mason Parks is Tyler Parks. But we have to be sure."

"No problem. It's fine. But what is the actual reason for your need to know?"

Sara goes on to tell me that there is a piece of land that belonged to Mason's father and his siblings. They had to contact all parties with an interest in the land because one of the heirs had made a claim, and all parties must sign off for it to be processed. She asked me to verify my address and said she would mail me the documents for my attention. We hung up, and I sat in continued shock before going back into the restaurant, where my family waited, feeling my exact same sentiment.

Stunned, we all agreed that we weren't hungry any longer and decided that it was time to go. Eli, Lela, and Andy looked at me with sadness and disbelief. We all drove to the restaurant separately, so we made our way to our individual vehicles. As I pulled out of the parking space, I noticed my son Andy coming up beside me.

"Mama, you good? Are you okay?"

"Yes, I'm fine. I'll be okay. Guess I got my answer."

"But are you alright to drive? You need me to drive you home?"

"No, honey, Mama is good. I just need to figure this out. I don't really know what to do at this point. But I'll be okay. Love you, Andy."

"Love you too, Mama"

My cell phone rings and its Eli calling to see if I'm headed home. He tells me that he would meet me there, instead of going back to work. He didn't want me to be alone after hearing such news. He knew how I felt about my dad. No sooner than I hang up with Eli, another call comes in.

"Mommy, are you okay?"

"Yes, Lela, I'm fine. Really.

"Are you going to call Grandma to ask her about this?"

"At this point, we haven't spoken since she left here and that was not on good terms. I really don't think it would be a good idea for me to call her right now."

Lela tells me that she understands and that she was headed to take lunch to her husband, Drew, who wasn't able to join us. I think that was all by design. God had to have wanted us all together in one location that was free from any distractions.

Mason wasn't my biological father! She kept that secret for over fifty years and then told the truth to a stranger. Selfishly. I can only believe that she was trying to block me from getting any type of inheritance from the only father I knew.

Unbeknownst to me, my precious daughter had called her Grandmother seeking answers. "Mommy, I just got off the phone with Grandma. She denies it all and said that you had no business having me to call her. She said if you have issues or questions for her, then you would need to call her yourself."

So, I did. That very next day, but she didn't answer the phone. She called back later. When I saw her number on caller I.D., my heart started to race.

I answered with a tone that was very dry, yet matter of fact, "Hello."

Speaking in a tone that was familiar, my mother responds, "Hi, you called so I'm calling you back. You want to know about your biological father?"

"Yes, who is it?", I asked not sure of where this was going.

"He's no longer here", she says, so I'm thinking at this point that there had been some mistake.

"I know that. He died five years ago", I say with almost a sigh of relief.

My mother then says to me, "No. He died years before that."

"Okay." As I still remain calm with my tone. "What was his name?"

"His name was Chaz! Your daddy never knew and I didn't want you to ever know either. I was never going to tell you, and I have never spoken to that person Lela said that you

245

talked to. Whoever called you is telling a lie on me. I have never spoken about this to anyone!"

Needless to say, I was not able to continue on the phone with my mother at that time.

EPILOGUE

The greater part of my life has been spent pouring my heart out to God without even realizing it. Life has taught me that my mother would never have responded to that letter the way I needed her to. Quite simply, she wouldn't get it! I just had to pray.

My experiences lately have taught me that prayer is just like a ride on a roller coaster. You might fall down on your knees, or find yourself in your sacred place as you put in a request to one you have never seen, but with whom you trust with all of your heart. Likewise, you stand in a line, waiting your turn for a ride that is designed to take you to heights you've never experienced. Once you get on that ride, you trust that you will arrive safely at the end of the journey. Similarly, you hope that your prayer will yield positive results.

What is common to both is the type of journey you will to take. The roller coaster ride will have highs and lows; fast paced turns and slow movement at times; drops that make you scream for dear life; but, you trust that if you just hold on, you will make it to the designated end without incident. Similarly, with prayer you will go through highs and lows and encounter situations that you make you feel as though you will not survive. But just hold on!

With that roller coaster, you might get a chance to choose the one who will ride beside you, but you normally have no idea who is in front of you or behind you if you enter the line by yourself. The one thing you all have in common is the expectation that you will make it to the end of the ride. With prayer, you may have someone on this earth who believes as you do. Mutual hopes and dreams. And then you may encounter a few who make it their point to do their best to block anything that appears to be going your way. As long as you know that the one who sits on high is in control, you need never worry about those desires of your heart. Just like you don't worry when you sit on that ride. You trust that the engineer who designed it, and the one controlling the ride, will do exactly what is necessary to make sure your journey is complete.

For me, I have had some highs and lows, and peaks and valleys my whole life, but this ride is one like no other. And because I know that there is always divine intervention, I yield, and trust and believe that there will always be a positive outcome.

The ride that started for me when I was a mere five weeks old, has had quite a few twists and turns. Unlike most, I have never felt the type of love and connection that one normally has with their mother. I used to think that there was something wrong with me. But it wasn't about me.

My mom wanted people to see that I was her little girl and that she was the one who made me pretty, and that she was the one who should get the praise for making me the way I was. She didn't understand why they couldn't see that without her, there would be no me, there would be no Rebecca!

Liza was the one who had to leave home in a hurry; she was the one who gave birth at a hospital in the city all alone and full of shame, rather than having the abortion she so wanted to have; so ashamed that she refused to give this little girl a name at the hospital; she was the one who had to find and subsequently marry a man just to give the little girl a name; she was the one who was forced to move miles away from her family hoping for her fairy tale to come true; she was the one who put up with years of verbal, emotional, and physical abuse just to provide a nice life for this little girl.

So, why did they all seem to ignore her. Why did everyone always seem to love Rebecca more than they loved her?

Didn't they understand that if things had been different, there would be no Rebecca!

That cute little girl, with the fat cheeks and dimples, who always had on the prettiest of clothes, and had the best of everything would not even exist if she had made a different choice.

The truth has finally been revealed.

My mother has *selfishly* lied to me for over half of a century; and her secret was kept by those who loved us both, by those who wanted to love me, and by those who were never allowed to even know me.

Mason was *not* my biological father.

Neither he *nor* I ever knew.

My biological father's name was Chaz.

He did know.

I have another mom.

She knew.

I have *my very own* sister and brother.

They knew also.

As did countless others.

And no one ever told.

Secrets.

Lies.

Not a movie.

My life.

I'm doing okay. I'm able to process it a lot better than before. As a matter of fact, I now find myself looking in the mirror in wonderment.

What I have done to be blessed in such a mighty way? Even though my heart has been broken by those I have always known, trusted, and loved, I have made it this far without long term emotional injury. I once felt as though I had been dealt a hand that was really unfair because of things that have happened to me, but I survived. And so will you.

As my new life begins to unfold, I am able to see things through a different set of eyes. My focus is totally different.

I *UNDERSTAND* that I don't have to prove myself to anyone anymore. I am no longer required to buy love, or beg anyone to pay attention to me. There are no conditions.

I *ACCEPT* the family who wants to know me, those who want me in their lives, unconditionally; something my husband had to help me understand, because my mother, without remorse or compassion has tried to convince me otherwise: "You don't have any idea what you're doing. You've chosen them over us. They didn't even want you. They didn't want to know you or have anything to do with you. If they did, why didn't they reach out and try to find you?"

I really do *FORGIVE* my mother, and I will continue to pray for her to one day find the happiness she longs for and to be blessed with the desires of her heart. She seems happiest when not in my company, so I have decided not to force a fit any longer. I've wasted too many years. We both have. I hold no grudges against my mother, nor towards any others who have wronged me in any way. For the pain that I have caused my mother because of my existence, I apologize sincerely. There is no need to go down that road again. Lessons have been learned and it's time to move forward and appreciate our time on this earth.

What a blessing to be given what I have always wanted; a life filled with sincerity and the heartfelt *LOVE* that I truly deserve. I have gained a whole new village. Increase.

I have let go of the hurt that has plagued me for so long; those sleeping dogs have finally awakened; and my new journey has just begun.

But GOD.

83253643R00156

Made in the USA
Middletown, DE
09 August 2018